What the Wind Can Tell You

SARAH MARIE A. JETTE

Other titles from Islandport Press

The Door to January by Gillian French
The Sugar Mountain Snow Ball by Elizabeth Atkinson
Azalea, Unschooled by Liza Kleinman
Uncertain Glory by Lea Wait
The Five Stones Trilogy by G. A. Morgan

What the Wind Can Tell You

SARAH MARIE A. JETTE

ISLANDPORT PRESS

ISLANDPORT PRESS

Islandport Press
PO Box 10
Yarmouth, Maine 04096
www.islandportpress.com
books@islandportpress.com

ISBN: 978-1-944762-41-4
ISBN: 978-1-944762-46-9 (ebook)
Library of Congress Control Number: 2017952157

Dean L. Lunt, Publisher
Cover and book design: Teresa Lagrange, Islandport Press
Printed in the USA by Versa Press

To my father, Anthony Aliberti, and all the words he loved.

1

This one was different. I knew it. Mama knew it.

It takes a certain kind of seizure to ruin a sunny Saturday morning—one that rolls in like thunder and flashes like lightning. This seizure made my lungs ache for my next breath, a breath I didn't realize I was holding. This seizure absorbed all the movement in the room, stole my strength and channeled it into its jerky, confused convulsions. This was the kind of seizure that stretches time as thin as a sliver, where the sirens echoing from blocks away tease and taunt because sound travels faster than an ambulance ever could.

Julian's arms flexed and pulled like a fly caught in a spider-web, desperate and futile and useless. His legs sprang and kicked the underside of the table, rattling the silverware and cereal bowls. Cups and plates danced erratically on the place mats. His foot slammed against the table leg. A glass of orange juice tumbled over the edge and onto the tile floor, creating crystal constellations. The pinwheel he was holding tumbled out of his hand and fell to the floor.

Julian gulped and gasped for air as Mama guarded his head. His eyes rolled back and his eyelids closed, as though he didn't want to see what was happening to his body.

I didn't want to see it either, but my eyes wouldn't turn away.

His body bucked against his seat, fighting to escape. His clothing pulled; the chair groaned.

Julian kept seizing.

Mama sang—like she hoped the rhythm of *"Duérmete Mi Niño,"* her favorite lullaby, would offset the chaos erupting inside Julian.

She sang louder and louder.

"Duérmete pedazo de mi corazón . . . "

She then broke into "This Little Light of Mine." Tears glistened on her cheeks.

Mama kept singing.

Julian kept seizing.

I watched her hands tremble as they stroked Julian's hair. They smoothed his curls; they fluttered and fussed as his head slammed and pulled against his wheelchair's headrest.

I counted the thumps of my heartbeat, hoping to lose myself in the numbers. I didn't, because Julian kept seizing.

His body continued to quake even as his arms and legs seemed to tire. They moved because they were forced to, weak and exhausted.

Mama's eyes flashed around the room—first settling on the clock, then locking on to mine. She opened her mouth to speak, but the words froze in her throat. All that came out was a squeak.

The stream of orange juice soaked into my socks, cold, wet, and sticky. I wiggled my toes, releasing my feet from the floor, no longer cemented by fear.

I pushed off my chair and pulled my mom's cell phone out

from her purse. My fingers searched for the buttons. I pressed the receiver to my ear. It started ringing.

"Nine-one-one. State your emergency."

"It's my brother. He's having a seizure. A big one."

Julian has seizures all the time. They come and then they stop. This one was different.

The dispatcher called for an ambulance, and I settled down beside Julian.

"*Cálmate, cálmate,*" I leaned in and whispered.

"This wasn't supposed to happen again," Mama said, and then she started to hum another song.

Julian's seizure stopped just before the ambulance arrived. By then his head was drooping like a sunflower in September. His arms and legs hung limp, like overcooked noodles.

One EMT pressed Julian's wrist to check his pulse. The other attached a foam brace around his neck. They slid a mask over Julian's mouth. Mama stepped between the EMTs to tuck a curl underneath the mask's rubber band. I kissed Julian on the forehead just before they carried him out of our house.

"I'll be back as soon as I can," Mama whispered. Her hug was tighter than usual. It seemed like her arms would never let go, but they did.

I saw Mama reach for her cell phone as she settled into the back of the ambulance. The doors closed and the ambulance sped away, lights flashing red and sirens screeching.

I sat on our front lawn and waited. My fingers tapped against my knees and I shivered. Big seizures filled me with jumpiness, jitters, and tears. Fortunately, Julian hadn't had a seizure this big in over a year. Seventeen months, two weeks, and four days, according to my mom.

Mama tracked all the seizures and ambulance visits thanks to her special gift. Ask her, and she'd tell you what number we were on. I could remember the length of some seizures, but Mama remembered the length of each one, even the smallest; she recalled the license plate number of every ambulance, and the names and eye color of all the EMTs, doctors, and nurses who had ever helped Julian. For Mama, remembering seemed to hold clues which might someday unlock the mystery behind Julian's seizures, once and for all.

A breeze swept the front yard. Sand on the driveway swirled against the curb. Fresh green leaves swayed hesitantly. I looked up at the sky, through the branches of our lilac, the blossoms now shriveled and brown. Closing my eyes, I took a deep breath to soothe my shaking arms, willing away the memories of Julian's seemingly never-ending seizure.

My ears caught the sound of flip-flops snapping their way across the street and sidewalk, followed by softer steps across our front lawn.

"Isabelle?"

My eyes popped open.

Jamie, the high school girl from down the street, stood before me, enveloped in the overpowering scent of powdered cheese. Her right hand presented me with a very full bag of cheese curls, while her left hand pressed her phone against her ear. I reached in and grabbed a handful.

"Hold on," Jamie said, pulling the phone away from her cheek.

A high-pitched voice chirped on the other end. Jamie stooped down and placed a cheesy hand on my shoulder. "You okay?"

I shrugged.

"The doctors will make things better," Jamie said. "They always do."

"It's been so long since the last time," I whispered, wiping my eyes on my sleeve. "I didn't think there would be any more big ones."

Jamie shoved the foil bag into her tote, gave me a quick hug, and followed me into my house. Jamie had been my babysitter for years and even though I was twelve now and could stay home on my own, Mama always called and Jamie always brought snacks.

Jamie found her old spot on our living room couch, nestled among the pillows. I watched her prop a chemistry textbook against her legs, wedge highlighters in the spaces between her toes, and press her phone up to her ear with her shoulder.

I swept the broken glass off the kitchen floor, sponged up the spilled juice, and wiped the table with a fistful of paper towels. With no more chores to do, I sat and stared out our kitchen window.

On warm afternoons, Julian sat on the back deck watching his wind socks snap at each other while his kites looped through the clouds. This morning, in between bites of cereal, we had been crafting pencil-top pinwheels. I drafted the plans, and with a thumbs-up, Julian had marked his approval.

And then the seizure had struck.

Far under the table, I spied Julian's pinwheel. The blades were soft and wet with juice. I blotted it with a napkin and pressed the pushpin deeper into the eraser. Once it was dry enough, I wrapped the pencil with colorful strips of tape. I placed the finished pinwheel on Julian's tray so it could dry completely.

I checked the time. It was only ten o'clock.

Inspired by Jamie's studying, I pulled out my science fair project and dumped the contents of my school bag onto the tabletop. For weeks, I had been extensively researching all things related to wind. In one book, I had found that New Hampshire's Mount Washington holds the record as the windiest place in the United States, with gusts reaching up to 231 miles per hour. My notebook was also filled with facts on weathervanes, including the Italian Gallo di Ramperto, the world's oldest rooster weathervane, which was more than 1,400 years old.

"Gallo di Ramperto," I whispered, letting the words roll off my tongue.

My favorite research find was a description of the octagonal Tower of the Winds in Greece. Sculptures of Greek wind gods encircled the top. Some looked like angels draped in cloth; the others looked like bearded men carrying jugs. I made Mama promise that we'd visit one day.

"Ancient buildings are rarely accessible," she reminded me.

"We can find a way," I said.

Sitting at the kitchen table with my notes spread before me, I pulled out my tri-fold presentation board.

"Hold on, let me call you back," Jamie's voice rang out. She left her phone on the arm of the couch and hobbled to the fridge, her highlighters still in place.

"You want anything?" Jamie asked as she poked around.

"Milk, please."

Jamie poured me a glass and took the last bottle of Papa's Jarritos soda. She delicately placed a handful of cheese curls next to me, licked her fingertips, and wiped them dry on her sweatshirt.

"Want anything else?"

"I'm fine," I said.

Jamie looked over my shoulder and read a few of my notes. "Is this for the McKinley Middle School science fair?"

"Yes," I said, watching her glance over my work. "My report is finished, but I feel like I need something else . . ."

"Like what?"

I pulled Julian's pinwheel off his tray and gave it a flick. The blades stubbornly refused to spin.

"That's what I've got to figure out. I've been making wind instruments for years, but now I feel like I want to try something more complex."

"Complex is good." Jamie nodded with approval. "So long as you have the research to support your project."

"I've got the research."

"I can tell!" Jamie smiled and took a swig of Papa's soda. "The winners go on to Regionals—even the seventh graders. And there's prize money, too, if you win Regionals."

"Really? I never thought about winning."

"Think about it, Isabelle. You're off to a good start."

"Thanks." I smiled.

She paused and took another sip of soda. "Did you know the Romans thought that reading the wind could predict the future?"

"I didn't know that," I said, looking up.

"Yeah, I read it somewhere." Jamie's phone began ringing. She returned to the couch, carefully adjusted her highlighters, and slipped her phone back against her ear.

The light in the kitchen windows changed from blue to orange to purple as the sun set and the sky grew dark. My stomach rumbled as Jamie finally finished her phone call. She microwaved some chicken nuggets, divvied up the last of the cheese curls, and poured us each a glass of juice.

Finally, the headlights from Mama's car flashed through the foyer.

I met her at the door with a hug.

Jamie patted me on my shoulder and walked home, the scent of cheese trailing behind her.

"It's a good thing your father's not here," Mama said as she sniffed the air. "You know how he is when he smells powdered cheese."

Dark circles rimmed her eyes, but I let out a sigh of relief. If Mama could joke about Papa, then Julian was okay.

We settled into our "Julian's at the hospital" routine. Papa swapped his late shifts at his store for the late shifts at the hospital so he could be Julian's night watchman.

It was one long week, seven days of dodged questions and too-brief hospital visits, before Julian could return home. As I was slipping into bed that Saturday night, I heard the rumble of Papa's car on the driveway. I barreled down the stairs to meet it. From the front door, I watched Papa scoop Julian out from his seat, carefully cradling Julian's head against his chest.

Papa carried Julian into the house like a firefighter, except for his bouquet of balloons trailing behind. Julian wasn't asleep but he didn't quite seem awake, his eyelids half closed, his arms pulled close to his chest. He was humming a song, and the cool spring breeze was making him shiver. His humming sounded like radio static.

I followed Papa as he brought Julian to his room, pulled off his jacket, and laid him on his bed.

"He's wearing those thin pajamas," Mama said. "I'll put Abuelita's quilt on the bed."

"Did you tell her?" Papa asked, his mustache twitching as his eyes caught mine.

Mama smoothed the quilt and shook her head.

Papa's shoulders sagged.

"I will," Mama said. "Tonight."

I wondered what it was they were keeping from me.

Mama tucked Julian in and Papa grumbled about closing up the store.

"Hernando, I ordered a pizza for you," Mama called out, never once taking her eyes off of Julian. "It's in the fridge."

Papa stopped to kiss me on the forehead and whispered in my ear: "Mmm, pizzawich."

From Julian's doorway, I watched Papa pull the pizza from the fridge and stack all eight slices. Looking back at me, he winked before he took an enormous bite. With his pizzawich in hand, Papa slipped out the back door and left for work.

I stepped into Julian's room and walked to his bedside, his

pinwheel in my hand.

"Julian, look what I finished for you. I didn't know what colors you wanted, so I put every color on this one." I curled his fingers around the pencil base, but his grip wouldn't hold. I wrapped my hand around his and blew on the blades. They refused to move. "I'm still trying to get it to spin," I apologized.

Mama placed her hand on my arm.

"He's very tired, Isabelle. Maybe tomorrow," she said.

I stood and tucked the pinwheel into the pencil cup on top of his dresser.

"Mama?" I asked.

"*Sí?*"

I turned back to my mother, who sat in her chair beside Julian's bed, stroking his face. She held his hands, gently flexing his knuckles. She pressed her cheek against his and whispered something softly into his ear.

"What if Julian has another big seizure?" I asked.

She closed her eyes and took a deep breath.

"That's not for you to worry about." She stood up, and began unpacking Julian's hospital bag. "I'll stay here for a little while, and when I go to bed, I'll be listening to the monitor. Time for bed, Isabelle."

"Good night, Julian," I said, and kissed him on his cheek. "I'm so happy you're home."

Reluctantly, I left his room. Each step felt monstrous, each one taking me farther away from Julian. In the kitchen, I hesitated. The soft smell of citrus filled the air. I peeked into Julian's room. The balloons were strangely still, but nestled in between stubby yellow pencils, his pinwheel spun in a blur of colors.

"Isabelle!" Mama called out, not bothering to turn around. Bat-like hearing was her other special gift. "Bed!"

I trudged up the steps and into my room.

Without Julian, the house had been so empty. Upstairs, alone in my room, Julian was still too far away. I sat on my bed, batting a basketball between my fingers, faster and faster. As my fingers raced, I listened for my mother. Close to an hour later, with my eyelids drooping and my cheek resting on top of my ball, she appeared in my doorway.

"Isabelle, it's time for you to sleep." Her smile was warm and her eyes were tired. Mama pulled the ball from my lap and placed it in my closet.

"I'm glad Julian's home," I said.

"Me, too." She sat beside me and kissed my forehead.

"He's better, right?" I asked.

"Yes and no." I searched her eyes for a clue as to what she meant, but Mama wasn't looking at me. "Julian can no longer be on the medications he was on before, so the doctors changed them."

"That's happened before." My words eased like a tiptoe, measured, soft, and balanced.

"It has."

"So, what's wrong?"

Mama placed her hands around mine. "Your father and I hoped that one day things would get better, that one day the seizures would go away. The big seizure last week showed us they're not going away easily. So, we're going to try something different, to try to get rid of the seizures once and for all."

"Okay . . ."

"Julian's new medication is strong, which is why we're starting off with a low dose."

"All right." I could tell she hadn't finished. Her lips were working with a silent thought, but her eyes closed, keeping the words trapped. "What if this new medication doesn't work?"

Mama patted my leg.

"That's not for you to worry about," she said again. Mama tucked her curls behind her ears and smiled. "The big surprise is that your *tía* is coming for an early visit."

"But it's not vacation."

"I know."

We sat in silence for a moment.

"Is that what Papa wanted you to tell me?"

"In part. Go to sleep, Isabelle. It's late." She kissed my cheek. "Everything will be all right."

Sliding under my covers, I pressed my head deep into my pillow. Tía Lucy had always visited the last week of June, for as long as I could remember. Something was up. I closed my eyes and tried to push away the worry.

And that's when the smell of citrus returned.

I pulled my blankets back and sat at the edge of my bed. I waited until the radiators quit clanging and the refrigerator stopped gurgling. I waited until Mama settled in her bed and her bedsprings fell silent. I waited until my heart slowed down enough that I could count its beats.

And then I tucked my pillow under my arm and tiptoed

down the stairs to Julian's room.

Julian's room was off limits. Mama and Papa didn't care that my room was a mess, so long as Julian's wasn't. His room housed all of his equipment: physical therapy toys and occupational therapy tools, pump parts, and suction machines. They didn't want me moving his noisemakers or mats, tangling his tubes, or misplacing his socks. I was only allowed in when Mama asked me to get something for Julian, or to check on him when he was resting.

That night, I stood in the doorway and peered inside. Julian's nightlight cast a soft blue glow on his bedroom floor. A gibbous moon illuminated his sleeping face. His room was perfectly still and orderly, even the bouquet of balloons tied to the foot of his bed and the pinwheel in his pencil cup. I sniffed the air and shook my head at my own silliness.

Julian's room was the same as always. And he was sleeping. His long eyelashes rested on his cheeks. He took a deep breath, turned his head toward the door, and exhaled. I walked over to his bed.

Julian slept in a hospital bed, specially delivered two years ago. Before the bed arrived, fluids used to clog his chest at night, and he wasn't strong enough to cough them out. Mama propped him up using pillows, but the pillows never stayed put. Papa worked the night shift at his store, but Mama worked the night shift at home. She slept in a chair beside Julian, suctioning fluids from his mouth like a dentist, repositioning the pillows when they slipped out of place. After a bad bout of pneumonia, Julian finally qualified for a hospital bed. Seven pillows and a curled-up towel were replaced by a single button. Sleeping in a hospital bed eased Julian's coughs. And best of all, it let Mama sleep through the night—sort of.

My eyes caught the red bead of light glowing from the monitor. As Mama slept, she listened to every crackle and buzz, every breath and turn that Julian made throughout the night. The slightest cough sent her racing down the staircase—wide-awake in half a second.

Lifting Julian's arm off his chest, I pried his fist open. The thumb was always the hardest. I slipped my hand inside his.

His breathing was steady and deep. His arm felt heavy. I kept his hand in mine as I pulled up Mama's chair and leaned my head against his mattress. My left hand skimmed the top of Julian's blanket, while my eyelids fell. My shoulders began to sag. His room was so tranquil, so serene. It was like all the silence in the world drifted into this moment.

Suddenly, the sound of stiff bedsheets startled me. I felt the quilt tug the back of my head, pulling my hair with it. Julian's hand squeezed tight around mine. I smelled oranges. I looked over to Julian's dresser. The pinwheel was spinning wildly.

And then I heard something I'd never heard before.

"Belle?"

Julian sat upright, his covers thrown back. His cheeks dimpled with an excited smile.

"It's almost time," he whispered.

"What?" I asked. My eyes blinked too fast, desperately trying to see what was right in front of me.

"You're coming with me, right?" Julian asked, his eyes widening.

"Yes . . . of course," I stammered, staring at his hand, marveling at its strength.

"Oh, good." His eyes never left mine. "I always hoped you'd join me one day, but I didn't think it was possible."

Julian pushed himself off his bed—without anyone helping him. He bent down and slid his feet into his slippers. Walking across his room, Julian reached behind his bedroom door and pulled his robe off its hook. I couldn't take my eyes off of Julian's feet—feet that had never supported Julian on their own. I tried to stand, but couldn't.

"Belle." Julian stepped closer and helped me up. He looked at me closely, his eyebrows deep with concern. "Are you okay?"

"You're talking! And you're calling me Belle?" I said, steadying myself.

"I'm talking because of Las Brisas, and I'm calling you Belle because I know you'd like me to."

"You remember me saying that?"

"I do."

I chewed my lips as I searched for my next words.

"Julian . . . you're walking . . ."

He smiled. "It's Las Brisas."

"What's Las Brisas?" I asked.

"You'll see," he said.

I watched Julian's arms as they slipped into the sleeves of his robe. His hands fluidly knotted the belt. He moved with delicate strength, like a butterfly as it approaches the inner petals of a flower. The room darkened as the moon arched past Julian's window. Shivers ricocheted from my head to the tips of my toes, but I stood still. And in that moment of stillness, I felt the brush of a breeze, fleeting like a memory.

"What're we waiting for?" I whispered.

"I never know, but it'll come soon." Julian paused at his dresser and admired his pinwheel. "I love the colors you put on it, Belle."

"Thanks. It's strange. It wouldn't spin for me."

"Las Brisas is spinning it," Julian said.

"Las Brisas is magic wind that helps you walk?" I asked, scratching my head.

"No, it's much more than that. Just wait and see." Julian pulled his dresser drawer open and reached in. "Here, put my sweatshirt on. The room is getting colder, and I have a feeling you'll want it."

In the glow of the nightlight, I watched Julian ball up his sweatshirt and toss it across the room. His aim was perfect.

"Nice toss." I couldn't hide the shock in my voice as the sweatshirt landed in my arms.

"Thanks." Julian's chest swelled with pride. "I've been practicing."

I raised my eyebrows.

When Julian's physical therapist visited, Julian lobbed beanbags at her. With a lot of focus and effort, he was able to pinch a beanbag with his right hand and hurl it toward her. This throw was entirely different. This throw was effortless.

Julian and I sat down on the edge of his bed. Once I'd pulled the sweatshirt on and rolled up the cuffs, he took hold of my hand. I leaned against him, my shivers rattling us both.

"I'm so glad you're here, but you've got to relax, Belle—otherwise Las Brisas won't come." He took a deep breath. I did the same.

I listened to our breathing. I felt the pressure of his shoulder against mine. I felt the soft breeze of the pinwheel. I watched the shadows in his room. They crept around his dresser, his stuffed animals, his wheelchair.

And then everything went still—the pinwheel, the sounds from the street, even the air around us.

From the edge of Julian's room, I caught a shimmer of light seeping out from under his closet door. It spread like ink.

In seconds, Julian's floor became a pool of radiating silver light.

"*Las Brisas vienen*," Julian said, standing and pulling me up with him.

Las Brisas was coming.

I hesitated, my other hand holding on to Julian's quilt, threads tying me down to reality. The light on the floor inched closer, reaching out for us. It saturated the fibers of the rug. My toes started to tingle.

Julian leaned in close.

"There's nothing to be afraid of, Belle." Behind him, small pillars of light reached up and illuminated his room like moon glow. "Please come; we have to hurry."

As if responding to his words, the light began creeping back to the closet. I saw the pinwheel begin to spin. I squeezed Julian's hand, he squeezed back, and we stepped onto the puddle of light.

The breeze returned as we inched toward the closet.

Julian pulled the door open.

"Where're we going?" I leaned in to ask.

"Las Brisas," Julian whispered.

The light snuffed out once we stepped inside the closet. The darkness was as deep and dense as black velvet. The breeze brushed against my cheeks, smelling of mud, horses, and French fries. I couldn't see the ground before me, so Julian led the way.

After several minutes of silent wandering, I spied red, neon-green, and blue lights cutting into the darkness. They spiraled and formed shapes. A large circle spun in the distance. The sound of organs and bells woke the air around us.

Julian suddenly turned to the right, where an archway stood before us, crafted from hay bales, cornstalks, and pumpkin pyramids. I knew those pumpkins. I had climbed those hay bales.

Julian and I were standing at the entrance to the county fair.

Hand-painted signs pointed to 4-H barns and livestock contests. Flashing lights illuminated dozens of rides, and the scent of fried dough teased my nose. Somewhere in the distance, I heard the steady drum of popcorn popping.

"Belle, what do you think?" Julian asked, his voice startling me.

"Is it real?" I asked.

"In a way."

"Julian," I said, looking down at his feet and across to the fairgrounds. "I don't understand what's happening."

"Come and see." Julian pulled at my hand, but my feet held fast.

The night sky was free of stars and without a moon. It was black as midnight in a cave. Even with the pulsing and glowing lights from the fair, the darkness hovered heavily above. I took a deep breath.

"Belle," Julian said, taking me by both hands and stooping down to hold my gaze, "don't worry. Everything's fine."

"What is this place?" I asked. It was definitely the county fair—my parents brought us every year, in the fall. And judging from the photos decorating the top of our fireplace, Julian had gone there years before I was born. The fair was exactly as I remembered, but also completely different. The smells were the same: goats, onion rings, hay. The sounds were the same. My ears buzzed with the tinny spring of arcade games and the moos and snorts from barnyard pens. But there were no people. The fair stood hauntingly empty. The contrast made me shiver.

Julian tightened the belt on his robe. "This is my place. It's where I go at night, every night. Come with me, Belle." Julian's voice ached. "Please, let's have some fun."

"You come here every night?" I asked.

"Not here to the fair, but to Las Brisas, yes. Well, there have been a few nights I missed. Like the week following my twelfth birthday when I had pneumonia."

"You were at the hospital for two weeks."

Julian nodded.

"On my sickest days I didn't go—too many hospital tubes holding me back." Julian pulled my chin up and looked into my eyes. "Come on, Belle. Let's have some fun."

My eyes got lost in his, in the warmth, in the love, in the longing.

"Can we go on the Banana Slide first?" I asked.

"Absolutely!"

Julian took my hand and together we raced toward the Banana Slide. This was always my first ride at the fair. Julian and I slipped through the metal gate and trudged up the steps. At the top, I snuck a peek across the fairgrounds. The roller coaster roared along its tracks. Horses' hooves thundered on the dirt racetrack, pulling empty harness carriages behind them. Buccaneer Bob's Pirate Ship plunged.

"Are you ready, Belle?" Julian asked, lifting two burlap sacks off a neatly folded stack.

"As ready as I'll ever be," I answered.

We laid the sacks down on the landing and took our positions.

Gripping the edge of the sack in my fists, I nodded.

"Three . . . two . . . one!"

We pushed off and flew down the slide, riding the curves up and down. My stomach flipped and flopped. As I leaned back, gaining speed over the final bump, I could taste last night's pizza rising up in my throat.

"Julian," I gasped once I reached the bottom. "Let's go on the bumper cars next!"

Julian stood up, gave me his hand, and pulled me to my feet. We raced down the dirt path to the next ride.

In the real world, Papa rode the bumper cars with me. The whole experience was miserable. No matter what we tried, year after year, we were trapped between the other riders. My car always steered as well as a Zamboni in a sandbox. Papa's car only gained speed when he rode backwards. It wasn't very fun.

This time, we had the entire space to ourselves. Julian maneuvered his car with expert accuracy, zooming up from behind, curling in front of me, or skidding away to avoid a crash. He let me hit him a few times, but always came on strong afterwards.

I was an easy target, as my mind wasn't in the game. I found myself lost in Julian's smile, so easy and so effortless—so much like Papa's on Sunday afternoons.

"Julian, I can't believe this is happening! I'm so glad I'm here with you," I said as our engines slowed.

"Me, too."

I stepped out of my car and reached for Julian's hand.

The Tilt-A-Whirl was next, followed by games. We threw darts at balloons, tossed rings onto bulbous clown noses, and fished for rubber duckies. When we were through, I awarded myself a six-foot-tall purple tiger. After that, we made our way to the small white barn with windows that glowed warm with light.

Without the crowd, the petting zoo was better than I

remembered. Chickens pecked around us, their downy feathers littering the wood-chip floor. Baby goats skittered past. A clump of lambs huddled in the farthest corner.

When we used to go to the fair in the fall, children chased the chickens, poked the piglets, and head-butted the goats. The animals were frantically fleeing the other children as Mama wheeled Julian into the corral. It didn't take long for the animals to realize how hard it is to nuzzle a child in a wheelchair. Julian wasn't able to stoop down low or lean far over to the side. The chair was cold and hard and smelled of cheap rubber. I tried to catch a bunny or a chick for Julian to hold, but I ended up looking like all the other kids running after animals that stayed just out of reach.

This time, it was different.

Julian knelt down on the barn floor while I sat beside him. My nose twitched, filled with the scent of sawdust and dander, feathers and fur. Julian reached his hand toward the animals. A bunny hopped over and nibbled on his fingertips. The lambs turned to watch. A white and gray goat, her belly swollen well beyond her rib cage, staggered over. She tugged at my sock with her front teeth. I laughed and pulled my foot away, startling the goat for a moment. I reached out and scratched her muzzle, right up to the spot between her tiny horns.

"Belle," Julian began. "This is the nicest time I've ever had here."

"I agree."

"No, Belle," Julian looked at me closely, his eyes clear and bright. "I don't just mean at the fair. I mean since I've been traveling to Las Brisas. It's been fun—but it's more fun with you."

I stopped scratching the goat and turned to him.

"You should've told me—"

I stopped. Julian's face changed, ever so slightly. His jaw set. He swallowed.

"You know I can't, Belle." Julian's words weren't harsh, but they were final.

I dropped my head. I'd forgotten about Julian, at home, in his chair . . . The Julian sitting beside me had stolen away all my memories. He moved so easily; his voice sounded like a song. I felt hypnotized.

Other animals came by to check us out: sheep, guinea pigs, a spotted duck. And pretty soon, they settled into sleep. An Angora bunny hopped over and curled up on Julian's lap; a male mallard nestled on top of my purple tiger.

"There's not much time left. Anywhere else you want to go?" Julian asked as he gently placed the bunny on a hay bale.

I pulled my sock back onto my foot. It was wet and warm with goat spit. Peering out of the barn's doorway, I saw the haunted house, the upside-down Ferris wheel, and Buccaneer Bob's Pirate Ship. Even with Julian by my side, none of those rides enticed me to take a spin. Then my ears picked up the chimes from the carousel. Julian's head cocked at the same time.

"Shall we?" he asked.

"Yes, definitely!"

Last September, Julian and I had gone on the carousel together for the first time. Mama carried Julian on board and propped him up in the corner of a bench. She didn't have her array of pillows, but she had her years of experience. Mama rolled her parka up like a python and wound it around Julian's neck. She sat me down beside him, and posed me like a department-store mannequin. My left arm hugged his waist tightly. Once she was satisfied, Mama kissed me on my forehead and marched over to the operator. She spoke quickly with only a few hand gestures, before joining Papa behind the fence.

When the ride began, it spun slowly—very slowly. The other riders looked around, afraid there was some sort of malfunction. We inched along and swung past the teenage operator. He gave Julian the look I'm very familiar with: looking at Julian while *not* looking at him. Once the grumbling of the other riders grew louder than the music, the operator cast one last glance at us, spun the ride a little faster, and then a bit faster still.

Julian's eyes were as radiant and bright as the lights they tracked. The disco balls in the ceiling scattered rainbow squares across his face. The music swelled and the ride slowed. When the carousel stopped, I waved the lanky teenager over and handed him the last of my tickets.

On our second turn, I didn't hear the music or see Mama and Papa slip in and out of view. I only watched Julian. His hair fluttered in the swirl of the ride. His eyes darted back and forth. He was so happy. My stomach twisted and I wished I had saved more tickets to share.

In Las Brisas, Julian and I stood watching the ornately painted horses glide up and down. When Julian opened the gate, the ride slowed down and stopped for us. I looked over my shoulder. There wasn't a fifteen-year-old at the controls this time. Like every other ride at the fair, there was no one at the controls.

"Which pony do you want?" I asked as we stepped onto the platform.

Julian's hands lightly traced the horses. He walked past a glittery blue unicorn, a brown spotted stallion, and a painted horse sporting a glazed cowboy hat. Julian stopped when his eyes settled on something a short distance away.

"Let's sit together on that bench," he suggested.

Julian walked me over to a silver bench, decorated with jewels, horseshoes, and golden butterflies. This time I sat in the corner and Julian sat next to me. I rested my head on his shoulder as the carousel started to spin. I watched the animals rise and fall on their posts, moving with the gears mounted high on the ceiling. I watched the lights flash and swirl. Leaning against Julian, wrapped in his sweatshirt, with the sound of his voice fresh in my memory, everything felt perfect.

And then, ever so slightly, the ride began to slow. All around us, the fair grew quiet. Rides stopped moving; lights quit blinking.

"What's happening?" I asked.

"It's time to go home," Julian said.

"Already?" My heart pounded in my chest. My hand gripped the side of the bench, turning my knuckles white.

"It's getting late, Belle." Julian's voice was soft as the sounds of the fair faded. "You need to go back to bed and get some sleep."

"But Julian," I said, looking into his deep, brown eyes, "I don't want to leave you."

Julian's hands folded over mine, warm like a fresh tortilla.

"You aren't leaving me. You're always with me back home."

The lights dimmed until there was only silent, still darkness. I closed my eyes and when they blinked back open, the darkness was familiar. We were back in his room. Julian lay behind me, in his bed. I slipped my fingers out from Julian's and massaged my arm. It felt as though the blood from my fingers had pooled in the crook of my elbow. My knees snapped as I stood up from Mama's chair and leaned over Julian.

"Good night, Julian," I whispered.

His chest rose and fell with measured breaths. I smoothed his quilt, pulled his sweatshirt over my head, and tucked it back into his drawer. I peered closely at the pinwheel. I blew on the crinkled blades and they refused to spin. My fingers moved in to pick it up. With goose bumps sprouting on my arms, my hand hesitated. I shook my head, and with legs still jittery from Las Brisas, I tiptoed out of his room.

As I slid into bed, I glanced at the clock.

It was 3:18 in the morning.

Mama woke me from a dead sleep, the kind where your head's too heavy to lift because your neck is still snoozing, the type of sleep where you've laid motionless for so long, your joints are locked and your body has sunk deep into your mattress. It was like I'd made a snow angel in my sheets, except my angel was caught in mid-motion, frozen in place.

When I opened my eyes, the lights were on, the curtains were pulled back, and Mama stood next to me with my blankets in her hands. She had a look of wonder on her face.

"I've been calling you for twenty minutes," Mama explained.

"I . . . I was having some strange dreams," I whispered.

Mama shook her head and dropped my blankets before returning downstairs. I peeled myself off my mattress, glancing briefly at my full-body imprint. I quickly changed out of my pajamas and then stumbled down the staircase. As my hand slid on the railing, I started remembering . . . Julian's voice, his smile, the look in his eyes. I hurried down the last few steps.

I loved Sunday breakfast. On weekday mornings, I had three jobs: pack my lunch, fix my own breakfast, and pour a perfect cup of *café con leche* for Mama. I did all that while Mama got Julian medicated, fed, and dressed for school. Any time remaining, Mama spent in the bathroom, slapping on makeup and tying back her curls before racing us out the door.

On Saturdays, our house was filled with physical, occupational, and other therapists. Papa worked a double shift while Mama and I spent the day coordinating all of Julian's appointments, and learning new tricks.

Sunday mornings were a weekly oasis. No therapists, no responsibilities. The house was free of well-intentioned professionals. On Sunday mornings, Mama spoiled me.

At the thought of food, my stomach rumbled. In all our excitement together at the fair, Julian and I hadn't eaten a thing. The smell of carnival food was ever present, but we'd never indulged. And that got me thinking about last year.

It had all been Papa's fault. He had an obsession with fair food—the type of love that a fresh tortilla has for butter. Fair food, in all its greasy glory, unleashed the part of Papa that Mama tried to keep hidden.

As a high schooler, Papa had worked part-time in the packaging department of an Oscar Mayer factory. When they discontinued their spicy pork rind–flavored dogs, Papa brought home caseloads and hosted a hot-dog-themed block party, complete with a speed-eating contest. One minute and twenty-four hot dogs later, Papa knew he was on to something. Later that year, he organized the first annual hot-dog-eating fundraiser at his high school. It took weeks to round up enough kids to compete, because after practicing at home for a few months, Papa was a head taller and fifty pounds heavier than all the other students.

In the end, Papa competed against the mayor of his town, the football coach, the police chief, and the senior lunch lady.

On that fateful March morning, standing before platters of steaming franks donated by the hot-dog factory, Papa finished off his plate in just under 120 seconds—two quick minutes. Papa had eaten sixty-five hot dogs and their buns. He finished it off with a large squirt of mustard. More than four hundred dollars were raised for the prom and Papa earned his nickname. Even now, in some circles, Papa is still known as *Chanchito*. Papa, never one to limit himself, branched out to local and regional eating challenges. It didn't matter what it was or how long it had been in the fridge, with stopwatch in hand, Papa gulped it down.

Years later, Papa met my mother at a local talent showcase. He demonstrated his speed eating (twenty-five beef tacos, five quarts of cottage cheese, and one gigantic watermelon, all swallowed in five minutes), while my mother recited the names and birthdates of the two hundred audience members, after glancing at the list only once. They tied for first place, and tied the knot five months later.

Once they were husband and wife, my mother helped guide Papa to more healthful hobbies. She allowed him one day of indulgent eating each year (not counting Halloween, Thanksgiving, and Christmas, since those are times when it's okay to over-eat, with all the chocolate, turkey, and tamales). Papa chose the county fair as his place to splurge. Before each visit, Papa mapped out his route, researching and rating the best dough fryer, the greasiest sausage griller, and the slushiest Slurpee mixer. When we reached the entrance to the fairground, standing under the hay-bale archway, Papa bowed with gratitude and led the way.

Last year, I devoured an entire fried Italian sausage—peppers and all (Papa ate four), I split a bucket of onion rings with Papa (he ordered three more for himself), I gobbled up a sugary piece of fried dough (Papa ate five total), and even though I was full, I topped off the night with a caramel apple (Papa asked for a peck—which only confused the young woman behind the counter; he ended up eating six).

While Papa and I chewed, slobbered, and crunched, Julian sat there beside us, his feeding tube pumping his stomach with the same old, same old, teased by the smells of carnival food and by my smacking lips. I loved every bite—even though that night, like every year before, I ended up curled on my bed, trying to sleep off a bellyache. My stomach gurgled loudly, but not quite as loudly as the moans coming from Papa in the bathroom.

In the kitchen, Mama sat right in front of Julian. The big black curls of her thick hair hid his face, but I didn't need to see in order to know what she was doing. Her movements were so practiced, like a reflex. Mama was attaching Julian's feeding tube to his belly.

I slid into my seat. My fingers tapped the tabletop. I ached for Mama to move out of the way. My eyelids twitched, but I was too afraid to blink. When the soft breathing of the feeding machine pulsed in my ears, I knew she was almost done.

I wasn't sure what to expect when Mama stepped away. Maybe Julian would start talking and reminisce about the fairgrounds. Maybe he'd wink at me and then retreat to his usual self. Or maybe he'd be propped up in his chair, greeting me with his morning smile, the same as always. With his feeding machine *harrumphing* in my ears and my stomach grumbling, reality sank in.

Mama finally moved away, revealing Julian. His hair was brushed to the side, his dark curls packed in a neat wave. Julian's tray was filled with bells, tension balls, and other toys, but his hands were folded on his lap. His head drooped on his neck and his eyes were closed.

"Is Julian asleep?"

Mama didn't respond, passing me a bowl of cereal and a spoon.

"*Gracias,*" I said.

"You're welcome."

I took a bite and looked back at Julian. His eyelids slowly opened. I swallowed.

"Hey, Julian," I said, sliding my cereal over, scooting to the chair right next to his.

Julian's eyelids twitched as he fought to keep them open. I searched his face for a smile.

"Did you sleep well, Julian?" I asked, again looking for some sort of acknowledgment.

"*You* slept well," Mama said.

"Yeah, sound asleep," I answered as I leaned in closer. I watched Julian's chest rise and fall with each breath. I lifted his hand and swept it across the toys laid out on his tray, ringing some bells, crinkling some paper.

"Julian . . . ," I whispered, tapping his shoulder. "Hey—Julian."

I leaned across his tray and waved my hand in front of his eyes.

From the basket beneath the table, I picked out his maraca and slipped it inside his open palm. With his hand in mine, we shook the maraca a few times. His grip didn't tighten and his arm felt heavy.

I leaned in closer and watched as his eyes closed.

"Julian, wake up." I shook his arm gently at first, then harder. "Come on, Julian. It's morning."

"Isabelle," Mama called out. Her voice wasn't angry, but held a warning. I let go of his arm, straightened my back, and scooted my chair over a foot. "Please eat your breakfast and give Julian some space."

"Why is he—"

"Isabelle, Julian is tired. It's his new medication." Her voice grew sharp as she sat down beside me and opened her yogurt. "Now, stop staring at your brother, stop bothering him, and eat your breakfast."

I felt my cheeks get hot.

"I wasn't trying to bother him . . ." I sloshed a few soggy spoonfuls of cereal into in my mouth. The memory of last night burned. I swallowed and gathered the courage to look back over at Julian.

I knew I had to be quick. I filled my spoon with cereal and guided it to my mouth. Chewing as casually as I could, I snuck another glance in Julian's direction. Just as my eyes caught his face—his long slender nose, his high cheekbones—his head straightened, his eyes blinked open, and Julian stared right at me—eye to eye. He looked at me with such deep concentration, I gasped. And just as suddenly, Julian closed his eyes and turned his head away.

My spoon took flight. It left my fingertips, flipped in the air, and crashed to the floor. In the same instant, my hand fell into my bowl of cereal, knocking it over and onto my lap.

"Isabelle, what is with you this morning?" Mama's voice trembled. I knew that voice. She was worried. But once she got a look at my face, she frowned and handed me a rag.

I was smiling.

That look was a sign from Julian. He couldn't talk to me. Of course he couldn't! But that look, those seconds that passed between us, told me everything. I checked the time. It was 8:32. I sighed. There were too many hours and minutes and seconds until bedtime.

I pulled the rag from Mama's fingers and sopped up the cereal. I was too late; it had already soaked into my clothes. But I didn't mind. My heart was beating too fast, my mind racing in circles.

Julian knew. I knew. Nothing else mattered.

"Pancakes or French toast?" Mama asked as she bent down, picked up my spoon, and slid a clean plate in front of me. I paused to consider the choices.

"French toast."

Mama pulled a loaf of fresh bread out of the pantry and began slicing.

"Isabelle . . ." She paused.

"Yes, Mama."

She turned to look at me. Her eyes were unsure, questioning.

"Do you remember if Papa put Julian's robe on him last night?"

I stole a quick look at Julian before answering. His hand still held his maraca, and his breathing was steady.

"Maybe," I said. "I . . . I don't remember."

Mama reached for the egg carton in the fridge. I closed my eyes as the image of Julian pulling on his robe flooded my memory. When she spoke next, it was more to herself than to me.

"His slippers were on, too . . ."

I tucked my head down, afraid that Mama would see my face glowing—burning with excitement.

"Have you finished all of your weekend homework?" she asked. Her eyes flashed between Julian and me.

"I just have my science fair project."

I lifted my plate and balanced it on my fingertip, spinning it slowly, like the merry-go-round. The plate reflected the ceiling light as it rotated around. And then I turned it on its side, my fingers pressing against the center. Using my thumbs, I turned the plate like a wheel.

That's when a breeze toyed with my hair, brushing it against my cheeks and pulling my curls away from my face. The faint smell of popcorn drifted past. My hands froze and the plate stopped its spinning. The air around me grew still.

"What in the—?"

"Isabelle?"

I put the plate back on the table and took a breath.

"I—I think I have a new idea, something to add to my project."

"Are you sure you have enough time?" Mama cracked an egg and tossed the shell into the trash.

"It's okay." I smiled. "Julian helped me with the research; he can help me with this part of the project, too."

She nodded and turned back to her cooking. The smell of cinnamon and vanilla filled the kitchen.

"Before you begin construction, Isabelle, I'll need help bringing the summer clothes out of the garage. I looked at the forecast and it will be warming up this week." She slid slices of papaya and pineapple onto my plate. I smiled.

"Why would I put his slippers on?" Mama said softly to herself.

And then, as urgently as the smoke detector in our kitchen, Julian's feeding machine started beeping.

Julian's eyes opened with alarm. I stood up and switched the machine off. I pressed the clamp, readjusted the tube connected to Julian's belly, released the clamp, and switched it back on. It all took about ten seconds.

"There you go, Julian," I said. He gave me a dreamy smile of thanks.

Mama had taught me how to work Julian's feeding machine when I was seven, when she thought I was old enough to help out. I was ready long before. After years of watching Julian seize, listening to the *beep, beep, beep* of his feeding machine, watching Mama and Papa juggle all that comes with having a kid like Julian, I wanted to help. I wanted to make Julian feel better.

Just as I sat back down, the machine let out one long, loud *beep* before continuing its measured pump.

Mama peeked at Julian and turned away. She had her "It's going to be one of those days" look on her face. My heart dropped. That look was always spot-on. Mama could sense the good days from the not-so-good days without fail. That was another of her special gifts—foresight.

"Look at this, Julian," I said, pulling my chair over and crinkling one of his foil balls. His drooping eyes slowly opened and his arm reached up. He clasped the ball in his right hand and rotated it between his fingers. I opened up a package of putty and rolled it around in my palms. "Want to help me with my project today?"

His mouth twitched. His eyes opened wide. Julian smiled and I smiled back.

"Feel this, Julian." I tucked the putty into his left hand and watched his fingers close around it.

Mama returned her full attention to my French toast and I brought my bowl to the sink. As I rinsed the bottom of my bowl, I froze. This time it wasn't a beep that I heard, but a muffled cough, a gag, a choked reflex.

"Darn it!" Mama shut off the stove and moved the frying pan to a cool burner. She sat down with a thud in my chair next to Julian. I knew the tone in her voice and I knew that cough. Julian was seizing.

Softly, to myself, I counted: one one thousand, two one thousand, three one thousand, four one thousand, five . . .

Mama relaxed. Her shoulders rolled back and I could hear her exhale just as I got to five.

"I'll mark it," I offered, as Mama wrestled with Julian's feeding tube.

"No, Isabelle. Don't," she said, as I stepped away from the table.

"I got it, Mama. Five seconds." I pulled Julian's notebook out from Mama's desk and peeked at the clock. I wrote "8:39 a.m." in one column and "5 seconds" in the other.

Mama pressed her cheek against Julian's and whispered softly to him. His head slumped deep into his collarbone. Julian was usually quiet after his seizures, but this one had put him back to sleep.

Mama stood up and returned to the stove, stopping first at her desk to check my notes. I took her place beside Julian and removed the foil ball and putty from his hands. It was easy enough, post-seizure. I took his left hand in mine and began massaging it, rubbing his fingers, loosening his muscles. Soon enough, Julian was snoring.

Mama was right. It was one of those days.

Julian's seizures were short but constant. Mama relented and we were in a relay race: one of us ran to Julian's side while the other marked the time. Papa checked the seizure notebook first thing when he got out of bed. He didn't say anything to Mama or me after he'd examined the pages; he just walked over to Julian and kissed the top of his head. Julian had a ten-second seizure moments later. By early afternoon, we'd filled up twenty-four lines in his seizure notebook.

Mama and Papa used to wonder about the causes of Julian's seizures, but they stopped trying to figure it out years ago. Even after scans, exams, the best doctors, and multiple medications, we still didn't know why Julian's brain acted the way it did. That Sunday, though, Mama was blaming the doctors.

"Therapeutic dose," she mumbled to herself.

After Julian had returned home from his big seizure, Papa had explained that Julian would be changing medications. The thing was, he couldn't switch meds overnight. It would take a few weeks before what the doctor called a therapeutic dose kicked in and we could count on reliable seizure activity. Until then, we wouldn't know what to expect from Julian's seizures.

Julian's medications were always changing. Sometimes his medications worked well, but he'd only be allowed to stay on them for a few months. If Julian stayed on them too long, they could hurt him in some other way—they were too strong for his liver, or they could be toxic to his kidneys. Other times, the medications just stopped working. Some medications made him cranky, or he got a rash, or something else. There was always something else.

Mama, Papa, and I took turns soothing Julian through each seizure. My science project sat unfinished. As the sun set, Julian's head sagged on his shoulders, Mama's face had grown progressively more pale, and Papa had stopped speaking altogether. He just shook his head slowly and tried not to let me see when he wiped his eyes.

"Inez, he's been home for just one day," Papa muttered.

"And he's been on the new medications for one week. The doctors said this might happen." Mama placed her hand on Papa's arm. "The day before he was discharged, Julian had sixteen seizures. Yesterday he had fourteen. Today he's had thirty-six. The doctors said that they would fluctuate—sometimes more, but gradually less."

Lost in a day full of seizures, it was only when Mama said it was bedtime that I remembered.

It was like waiting for Christmas morning. I kept my door open a crack, so I could listen to the house. I pulled on my flannel pajamas in case Las Brisas was cold. I heard Mama click off the TV and the lamp beside the couch. I heard Mama's and Papa's feet padding into Julian's room. Then the whole house was still and silent for a few minutes. I pictured Papa brushing Julian's hair softly with his fingers. I pictured Mama sitting next to Julian, watching him sleep, singing a lullaby.

On their way out of his room, they switched on the monitor. Mama started up the steps first, singing the lullaby softly to herself. The words streamed up the stairs and crept into my room. I covered my head with my blankets and took a deep breath. Papa pushed my door open a little ways and watched me for a moment. I pictured Mama clicking on the receiver on her nightstand and listening closely for a few minutes to make sure it was working correctly, listening for Julian's breathing and the scratch of his blankets. I heard Mama and Papa slide into bed and then . . . silence.

Curled up under my covers, I told myself that I would count

to one hundred to be extra sure that Mama wouldn't hear me.

One, two, three, four, five, six . . . It felt like I'd never reach one hundred. I peeked out from under the covers and decided that fifty would be good enough. Seven, eight, nine, ten, eleven . . . Fifty never felt so far away. But it came, slow and steady.

Carefully pulling back my blankets, I crept to my bedroom door. I walked down the staircase with my hand gliding against the railing. At the bottom of the stairs, the rising moon illuminated the kitchen.

Julian's head was turned away from the door as I stepped into his room. His arm slid from his chest and dangled off the side of his bed, like he was reaching out for me. A passing car's headlights streamed through the room, placing a moving spotlight on his wheelchair, his feeding machine, his tools.

I suddenly felt embarrassed and silly. What if last night was only a dream? There I was, sneaking into my brother's bedroom in the middle of the night. Completely ridiculous! But then I remembered Mama's confusion about his robe and slippers.

And I smelled oranges.

Julian turned his head toward the doorway, as if inviting me in.

I let the darkness of Julian's room surround me as I tiptoed over to his bed. Holding his hand tightly in mine, I sat down on Mama's chair. Forgetting to blink, my eyes searched his room until my vision got fuzzy. Finally, I let my eyelids droop. I remembered the lights at the fair, as bright as fireworks glowing in the ebony sky. I remembered the sounds—the music humming from the rides and games, the horses' hooves thumping against the dirt track. And I remembered Julian's hand holding mine.

My arm, pressing the side of Julian's quilt, had fallen asleep. Just as my fingers started slipping out from Julian's, his grasp tightened around mine. It was so soft, so subtle and slight, I wasn't sure if I had dreamt it. I turned around.

Julian's eyes glittered.

"Are you ready?" he asked.

"I wasn't sure you'd come back." Julian's voice was soft. My ears strained to hear his words, clinging to each syllable.

"Why wouldn't I?" I asked.

"Today was rough," he said.

Julian slid off his bed and we sat together on the floor. His eyes scanned the room quickly, lingering on the pinwheel, and then he turned back to me.

"I'm glad you came. Las Brisas should be here soon."

"Julian, I've been wondering," I whispered, "why do you call it Las Brisas?"

"Because it blew in like the wind for months. Just a breeze coming from my closet, or from under my bed. I was too young and afraid to do anything at first. But it grew stronger, and so did I."

We sat in silence for a few moments. I harvested the memory of his voice.

"Do you want your robe?" I finally asked.

He shook his head.

"Mama put me in my flannel pajamas," he answered. "And we don't have much time."

"How do you know?" I looked around searching for a sign.

"Shhh," Julian hushed. "It's coming."

The light on Julian's monitor dimmed and darkened. The

pinwheel slowed its spin as his bedroom walls faded away.

Something wriggled beneath my body. I turned to Julian. "Belle!"

I shot to my feet, pulling Julian with me. The rug began to bubble underneath us. The furniture rattled and jerked, scraping against the floor. And then, as though someone had pulled the plug in the bathtub, the center of Julian's carpet spun and spiraled, dropping into the floor. The center grew wide, like the eye of a hurricane.

Julian's grip tightened around my hand. We fell on our bottoms and circled the room. The spinning grew stronger as Julian and I whipped around and around before plunging into the eye and falling through the floor.

Suddenly, water enveloped me. My arms flailed around in panic. Thankfully, Julian's fingers were still intertwined with mine. My eyes opened to see blurry blue light. Julian tugged on my arm, and I kicked my legs as hard as I could. With one last jerk, and one great kick, I reached the surface.

Coming into such bright light hurt my eyes. Everything was blue: the sky, the water, even the beach far off in the distance, fading into the horizon.

While I tried to make sense of our surroundings, Julian swam circles around me.

"Where are we?" I asked, salt burning my lips.

"In the ocean," Julian said, waving his arm out to his side to show the expanse of water all around us.

"Thanks," I said. "But I meant more specifically."

We had to be someplace tropical. The air was hot. The water

was as warm as the sunshine. The trees on the not-too-distant shore were lush and viny.

"We're in the Gulf of Mexico. And that"—Julian nodded his head toward the beach—"is Mexico."

"Mexico? How do you know?"

"I come here a lot. This is one of my favorite places." Julian ducked his head underwater and popped up beside me.

"How many places have you been to?" I asked.

"I don't know . . . more than I can count." Julian leaned back and started floating.

A breeze brushed against my face. The smell was unfamiliar but comforting. It smelled of never-ending sunshine, of freshness, of warmth. I watched a pelican fly overhead. Taking a deep breath, I turned back to Julian.

"When your room starts to change, do you know where Las Brisas will be taking you?"

He shook his head.

"It's always a surprise. I go to places I've been to or have been told about. I visit my favorite places the most."

"You can't choose?"

"I haven't tried. I just go where Las Brisas sends me."

"And when did you learn to swim?" I asked, marveling at his stroke and form. Julian looked at me and raised an eyebrow.

"In Las Brisas."

When Julian talked about Las Brisas, it sounded like fantasy, like a magical force of nature, like a dream. But there was no denying the reality of the water around me.

Julian floated by, gazing up at the clouds. Drops of water

curled around his nose, gliding down his bronze cheeks. His face grew more serious. I swam in closer.

"I like the ocean, Belle. I like the way it feels around my body. It lifts me up and carries me with it."

I flipped onto my back and floated with Julian, trying to remember if he had ever floated in the ocean before. The sun warmed my belly through my soggy pajamas. Julian reached out for my hand. With the sound of the ocean in my ears, the sun on my face, and Julian's fingers interlaced with mine, the world seemed perfect. I wanted to live in this moment forever.

"Belle," Julian said, pulling me in closer, "I want to show you something before time runs out. Come on."

He let go of my hand and swam to the beach. I followed.

The waves gently pushed us to shore. Water dripped off our pajamas, leaving a trail behind. Under the shade of the trees, I saw a path worn down by footsteps—Julian's footsteps. Julian reached for my hand again as he led me down the trail. The air soon became thick and muggy as we walked farther from the ocean. Beads of sweat dripped down my forehead. Mosquitoes hovered, but didn't bite.

"Look, there are the mangroves." Julian pointed up ahead.

In the soft, wet, and spongy soil, the roots of the mangroves coiled like tangled rope. Root bulbs bulged above the soggy earth. Just as my feet began sinking into the mud, Julian's path turned into sliced stumps. The mangroves grew thicker. Blue crabs poked their long thin antenna eyes out from tiny holes beneath the roots, scuttling sideways from one hole to the next, creeping in quickly. I felt the presence of birds tucked between the leaves, but couldn't see or hear them.

"Where're we going?" I asked as the path took another turn.

"Just wait and see." Julian's voice sounded excited, and his pace quickened.

The canopy of mangroves and vines hid the sun. I could scarcely see the sky above us. And then, just as I was starting to wonder when we'd ever get to the end of the path, it opened up. The branches seemed to pull back, revealing a tranquil pool edged by stones and surrounded by vines. It was beautiful.

"What is this?" I asked.

"A *cenote*."

"A what?"

"It's a cenote. It's what the Mayans called a pond with fresh water for drinking."

We walked to the edge of the path. The stumps turned into strips of wood, like a dock leading out over the edge of the water. Julian sat down, and I sat beside him.

"Is it deep?" I inched my leg down so the tips of my toes grazed the surface of the water.

"This one is. I don't know how deep, but every time I dive down, I can't find the bottom."

My fingers curled around the edge of the dock. The jungle air seeped into my lungs.

"How did you find this place?" I asked.

Julian shrugged. "Papa told me about it."

"Really?" I whispered. "He never told me."

"Well . . ." Julian paused to think. "Papa and Mama came here before I was born. There's a picture of them swimming in this cenote, on the mantel over the fireplace. Papa showed it to me when I was very little."

The water chilled my toes as I worked to remember the photos. I could recall the front few, but the ones in back were a mystery to me.

"I've never seen it," I said, shaking my head.

Julian must have sensed the jealousy in my voice. He leaned in and smiled.

"Belle, they're not keeping it a secret. Go see for yourself when we get back home."

The sun wrapped itself around my shoulders. Julian leaned in even closer.

"Cenotes like this one are connected by caves. If we swim to that far side"—he nodded across the water—"there's a passageway underneath the mangroves."

I squinted across the cenote. The water was completely still. I pulled my legs in close to my chest.

"Is there anything living in the water?"

"Some really small fish. Oh, and maybe a few sea monsters," Julian said, standing up and winking. He swung his arms out at his sides, preparing for his jump. Before Julian moved to the edge, I dropped in. The water was cool against my skin. My feet kicked and kicked; I couldn't feel the bottom.

Julian took a step back, leapt forward, and cannonballed into the cenote.

"How often do you come here?" I asked, when he popped up beside me.

"Once a month or so. Follow me!" Julian started swimming.

"This next cenote is amazing."

We swam to the far edge. Julian slowed and looked around the rocks and under some roots, deep in thought. His hands felt along the moss. He turned back to me with a satisfied smile.

"The passageway to the other cenote is here. I'll go first. You have to swim down about three feet, and then you'll get to the tunnel. Feel the stone above you. Kick your feet and pull yourself along the stone. When you don't feel it anymore, swim up and you'll come to the surface. I'll be there waiting for you."

I swallowed hard, looking deep into the water.

"Are you sure it's safe?" I finally asked.

"Don't worry, Belle. We're in Las Brisas. You'll be fine."

And with that, he plunged underwater and was gone.

Once Julian had slipped out of sight, the cenote was as still as glass. I felt the breeze on my face. I counted ten rapid heart-beats and then took the deepest breath I could.

Pulling myself under, I saw the black tunnel in the shadows. I felt the rocks encircling it, and then I swam into the darkness. My lungs screamed—not for air, but out of fear. My hands grasped the crags and jagged cuts in the stone. My feet kicked. My eyes stared into a vacuum of darkness. I swam farther and farther, down, down, down. And just when I thought the tunnel would never end, my hands wrapped around the edge of the stone. I kicked my legs as hard as I had ever kicked. It felt like minutes, it felt like hours, but it was actually only a few seconds later when I bobbed to the surface.

A small hole in the ceiling above let in a shred of light, slicing through the thick air inside the cavern. Bats fluttered overhead, their small wings flapping and snapping. The water was deep turquoise and crystal clear.

Julian sat on the hard stone shore, his legs crisscrossed, his smile broad.

"Incredible, isn't it?" he asked.

"It's beyond incredible," I said. The ground was cool against my feet as I stepped out of the water. "This is the most amazing place I've ever seen. It's like a cathedral."

The limestone walls were sculpted by time and water. A few sleepy bats dangled from the ledges. Vines fell from the cliffs like streamers.

Julian cleared his throat. "I like the way my voice echoes inside this cave. The sound bounces off the walls, the water, the stones. It must drive the bats crazy, but I love the way it makes me feel—all those vibrations."

I leaned back. My wet hair clung to my pajama top.

"Julian, can I ask you a question?" I felt my voice echo softly, encircling us, trickling down the stalactites.

"Of course," he said.

I gathered my thoughts. The bats slowed their flying and hung in frozen clusters at the top of the cavern.

"What's it like, when the seizures come?"

Julian's eyes closed. His eyelashes fluttered as he looked inside. "Numb . . . quiet . . ."

He slowly opened his eyes and looked up. The bats started flying again.

"Does it hurt?" I asked.

"No."

"What about after?"

Julian took a deep breath and ran his hands through his curls. "When the seizure passes, I'm tired. Very, very tired."

"You were tired today."

"I know," Julian said.

"It's the new medicine."

"I know," he said again. His voice was a whisper.

The light pouring into the cenote began to fade.

"Is it time to go?" I asked, standing up. "We just got here." My heart raced, and my mouth ran dry. The flapping of the bats' wings grew louder, the cenote darkened, and the water pulled farther away.

Julian stood up.

"Time is different here. Sometimes my visits to Las Brisas feel like hours, sometimes just minutes. There's little warning. When time's up, it's up."

His voice was warm and soft. It felt safe against the heavy darkness. The echoes of the cavern drummed in my ears. I felt Julian's presence beside me as everything faded to black.

Before heading back upstairs to my room, I pulled a chair up to the fireplace. In the rows of framed photos, tucked way in the back, I found a small picture of Mama and Papa swimming in the cenote. It looked just as it had moments ago. The mangroves just as thick, the water just as still. Mama's hair was parted in the middle and hung in two long braids that floated in the water like sea serpents. Papa's mustache was extra thick and covered his top lip as he smiled for the camera. His arms and belly were gigantic. I wondered if they knew about the passageway to the cavern. Even if they had, judging by the size of Papa's belly, there was no way he could have fit inside the stone tunnel.

The following morning, I slept through my alarm and was woken up when Mama called for me. I scrambled into my clothes and raced down the stairs.

Papa was pouring Mama's perfect cup of coffee. I watched him measure out the sugar, give it a stir, and sneak a sip.

"Papa, why are you still home?"

"*Buenos días,* Isabelle." He smiled. "I decided to leave a little later so I could see Julian off for his first day back at school."

I walked over to Julian and placed my hand on his shoulder.

"Good morning, Julian," I said. His head straightened, but then fell to his left shoulder. "Asleep again?"

"Isabelle," Papa whispered. I looked up, and his eyes darted to my mother.

Mama stood at the sink, busy cleaning Julian's feeding tubes. With her back turned, Papa took another sip of Mama's coffee, tiptoed to the fridge, and opened the door.

"Close it!" Mama snapped, without turning around.

"Inez, I was just getting something for Isabelle," he protested.

"You already did." Mama pointed to the bowl of cereal on the table. "Don't try to fool me."

Even though Mama had weaned Papa from his competitive eating years ago, Papa regressed whenever Julian had a hospital stay. When Julian came home, Chanchito returned. Like a little piggy, he made it his job to clean out the fridge—not with sponges and

wipes, but by eating anything he could when Mama wasn't looking. In years past, I had caught Papa slurping down condiments,
like balsamic dressing and mayonnaise, or gorging himself with
long-lost leftovers edged with furry green mold. Chanchito didn't
care. Because of this, Mama kept careful watch over the pantry
and the grocery bill. She replaced broken bathroom scales and
enacted daily weight checks. But Papa's hunger was unstoppable.

He snapped the door closed and paused for a moment.

"Papa?" I began, sliding into my seat.

"Yes, Isabelle?" He turned around slowly, slipping a garlic
bulb into his pocket.

"Why didn't you tell me about the cenote?"

Papa raised an eyebrow.

"What cenote?" he asked.

I tucked my hands under my thighs and looked at Papa
closely before continuing.

"The cenote you and Mama went to before Julian was born."

Papa looked at me like he wasn't seeing straight. Maybe he
was wishing he was at work. Papa's eyes shifted from Mama,
to me, and then settled on Julian, who sat in his chair by the
kitchen sink, fighting to keep his eyes open.

"I haven't thought about that place in years," Papa began.
"Right after Julian was diagnosed . . . those were the nights I
walked around the house with him in my arms, and I'd just talk.
I started telling him stories, and I told him about our trip to see
Francisco and Luis when your mother was pregnant. That's when
I had the ceviche-eating contest, right, Inez?"

"Yes, I remember," Mama said, looking up and rolling her

eyes, Julian's tubes squirming like jellyfish in her hands.

"Seven bowls of ceviche in under two minutes. Not my best record, but it was too delicious. I had to slow down to enjoy it." Papa smiled and patted his stomach.

"Tell Isabelle what happened after you ate all that ceviche," Mama said, reaching for her mug of coffee.

"She doesn't need to hear about that," he grumbled.

"Oh, yes she does." Mama sighed and continued. "Isabelle, what your father is hiding from you is that, yes, he ate seven bowls of the world's best ceviche in less than two minutes. But what followed was seven hours of throwing up."

"Yuck."

"Yes, Isabelle. Yuck."

Mama patted Papa on the shoulder. For a moment, his eyes looked far away, lost in the memory of the ceviche and its aftermath. And then, Papa turned and kissed Mama on her forehead.

"Inez, remember the butterflies at Teotihuacan?"

"How could I forget?" Mama turned to me. "After your father recovered, we traveled to the ancient city of Teotihuacan and climbed the Pyramid of the Sun."

"You climbed, I crawled," Papa corrected.

"Yes, that's right." Mama smiled. "It was a nice reward for our effort, seeing the butterflies at the top of the pyramid."

"Why?" I asked.

"Well . . ." Papa paused for a moment. "*La Pirámide del Sol* is over two hundred feet tall. Butterflies were the last things we expected to see once we reached the top."

"But that's what we saw, Isabelle. Dozens of butterflies,

spinning in circles at the top of the pyramid," Mama concluded. "It was magical."

Mama reached into Julian's basket and placed a sheet of bubble wrap on his tray, placing his hands on top of it.

I cleared my throat. I wasn't finished.

"You told Julian about the cenote. Why didn't you tell me?" I asked, my voice softer than I wanted.

Papa returned his eyes to mine and took a deep breath.

"I'm sorry, Isabelle. I just forgot about it. So much has changed in our lives. Those old memories were just pushed aside. Sometimes I forget that those moments even happened."

"Isabelle," Mama began as she sipped her coffee. "How did you learn about the cenote?"

"Julian told me," I said.

Papa's left eyebrow, the extra bushy one, raised up high. He turned to my mom and they both stared at me.

"Julian told you?" he asked.

Mama stepped closer and placed her hand on my forehead. I shook her off.

"I'm fine," I said.

"But Isabelle, Julian can't . . ." Her voice trailed off as she looked at Julian, his shoulders pulled down at his sides, his eyes half open and unfocused.

I wanted to ask more, but with the way Mama and Papa were looking at me, I thought it best to leave well enough alone. I poured milk into my bowl of cereal and dragged my chair over next to Julian.

"Come on, Julian, let's pop these bubbles," I said.

After school, I dragged my science fair equipment and research out of the kitchen, down the back ramp, and into the garage. It took a few trips, but was totally worth it. Our garage wasn't attached to the house, and didn't really have enough space to park our cars, so Papa and Mama used it for storage.

I left the door open for some air—it got too stuffy otherwise—and placed a sheet of plywood over a stack of plastic bins, creating a large work surface I wouldn't have to clear off at dinnertime. Less than a week before the science fair, I needed to think big.

I tugged my science notebook out of my backpack. On one page was a sketch of the merry-go-round from Las Brisas. I left off the animals and benches, but drew the circular base attached to gears and chains, which were all connected to a motor. On the next page was a sketch of a bicycle—two vertical wheels connected with gears and chains to a different power source: a wind turbine. The turbine was a larger model of the pinwheels Julian and I had already constructed.

In my sketch, large cardboard blades spread open at the top of the wind turbine, like a proud lily. I imagined the wind blowing the cardboard blades, not only spinning them, but also pulling a belt attached to the two bicycle wheels.

I yanked my toddler bike from its hook. Rummaging through

barrels of recycling, I found some large sheets of cardboard.

In a box labeled *Isabelle Birthday*, I unpacked a stack of plastic cups. Mermaids swam along the edges. My fifth birthday party had been mermaid-themed, and Mama had accidentally ordered two hundred cups instead of twenty. As a joke, Papa brought them out each year for my birthday celebration. Because my birthday parties were usually small, I assumed I'd celebrate my mermaid birthday into adulthood.

Using a yardstick and sidewalk chalk, I drafted blades for my turbine onto sheets of cardboard. With a hammer and a nail, I punched small holes into the sides of four cups and started to thread shoelaces through the holes.

Mama's car crawled up the driveway and pulled up close to the open side door.

"What's going on in there?" she said as she got out of the car.

"I'm making a turbine for the science fair."

Mama nodded absently.

"Your table is on top of the summer clothes."

"Sorry," I said, peeking underneath. "I'll be done by the end of the week."

Mama opened Julian's door and eased him into his chair.

"Hey, Julian," I called out as Mama wheeled him over.

"Let me see your plans," Mama said.

I spun the notebook around to face her. Mama explored the images, measurements, and notes while I studied Julian's face, breathing, and posture.

"How was his day?" I asked.

Mama looked over at Julian.

"He's still adjusting to being home." She patted his hand. Julian stirred, but his eyes remained closed. "It was a long day for him, even though his teachers took things slowly."

She started wheeling Julian toward the house.

"Mama, can Julian stay out here with me?" I called out.

"Isabelle," Mama said, turning around. I knew that look on her face. It was the post-hospitalization look, the overly cautious, Julian-might-break-again look. Fine lines appeared on her forehead, while the skin under her eyes grew puffy.

"Did he have a lot of seizures today?"

Mama shook her head.

"No, not many. He's at seven."

I adjusted my ponytail. She looked toward the house.

"For a little while?" I pleaded.

Mama looked at me, down to my notebook, and then over at Julian.

"You've got him for ten minutes." She kissed Julian's cheek.

"Only ten?"

"Don't push it, Isabelle." Her voice was guarded. "Be sure to call if you notice anything."

"I will." I pushed Julian beside the table and heard the kitchen door close behind me. Even though his eyes were closed, I bent down so our eyes were level and my words came close to his ears.

"All right, Julian. This is what I've got so far: cardboard turbine blades, my old bike, shoelaces, mermaid cups, and . . . now I need some sort of belt."

I tipped the plywood off the bins of clothing and pulled out a T-shirt. Using Mama's lawn shears, I cut the bottom off, creating a three-inch-wide loop.

"Julian. Julian, can you hear me?" I put my hand on his and watched his face. "Can you hear me through your sleep? Let me tell you my plan. I'm going to use this fabric as a belt. When it's wrapped around the wheels, it will spin and work as a pulley."

I leaned on the bike to hold it in place as I pulled the fabric into position. Reaching for Julian's hand, I placed his palm on the fabric belt and gave the wheel a gentle spin.

"See, Julian? The wheels are pulling the fabric around. Next, I need to find a way to secure these cardboard blades to the axle. When the wind blows, they'll move the wheels and then the belt."

I reached for Julian's other hand. I waited a moment, my eyes on his sleepy face.

"Julian?"

He exhaled. I shook his wrist. "Was that a *yes* exhale or just an exhale?"

Julian inhaled and exhaled.

"Come on, Julian." I stroked his hand. I lifted a cardboard turbine blade and fanned his face, blowing his curls up and everywhere. His breathing changed, adjusting to the force of the wind. His head turned back and his arms lifted up.

"Julian, wake up," I urged as I fanned him harder. Finally, his head pulled up and his left eye peeled open. When he saw me, he smiled. I smiled back.

"Julian, feel this." I moved the pulley once again. His fingers reached for the moving fabric. "I'm planning on attaching some mermaid cups to the belt, so when the turbine moves, it will scoop up something—like popcorn for Papa."

I watched Julian's hands for a thumbs-up sign. His fingers moved into a fist, and it looked like his thumb was trying to move out of his hand, but before he gathered enough strength, his arm fell to his lap.

"Oh, Julian." I put my project down and knelt beside him. His mouth twitched into a tired smile, but he held my gaze. "I think the engineering will work. I want it to do something useful, but fun. I don't think I have enough time, but wouldn't it be cool if I attached it to my old scooter so it could move with the wind? What do you think?"

Julian's thumb uncurled from his fist.

"Isabelle, time is up!" Mama called through the kitchen window.

"Thanks for listening to me, Julian," I said, as I wheeled him up the ramp.

Mama met me at the door. Her eyes scanned Julian from top to bottom.

"Everything okay?" she asked, in a voice that made me wonder if everything was.

"Yeah, I guess," I said.

"What do you mean, you guess?" She squinted and squatted, checking Julian from all angles. "You know we don't guess with Julian."

"I—I didn't mean . . ." I turned my eyes to Julian. "He's fine, Mama. He just—he just seems tired."

"That's fatigue, Isabelle. It's the side effect that I told you about. Remember?" She looked at me and then back at Julian. "No seizures?"

"You know I would have told you."

"I'm just double-checking."

"I would have told you and marked it in the notebook," I said, my voice softer.

Mama nodded, more to herself than to me.

"Forty minutes until dinner; you coming in?"

I shook my head.

"I've got to construct some more."

"Sounds good." Her eyes returned to Julian. "Julian's had only seven seizures today. It's early, Isabelle, but maybe this means that the medicine is starting to work." She bit down on her lip to keep from saying too much. "I've got to finish making dinner."

I nodded. The screen door snapped shut as I returned to the garage.

I tied the mermaid cups to the fabric loop. Once they were secure, I affixed my bike to my worktable using duct tape. I slipped the blades onto the axle on the rear wheel and gave it a test spin. The blades lasted two seconds before they wiggled their way off the axle.

"Humph."

With my fingers pressed against the blades, they stayed put, but every time I moved my hand, they flew off like maple seeds. I tried a wad of duct tape, but it didn't stick right.

"Hey, what about . . ." I turned to where Julian had sat, the space as empty as an echo. I left my supplies in the garage and ran into the house.

"Julian," I called. He blinked slowly as I approached. "I need something to hold the turbine blades down, something like . . ."

Inside his basket I saw a tub of putty. I pulled it out and waited for his thumbs-up. Julian looked at me with dreamy eyes and blinked slowly, like a satisfied cat. I leaned in and kissed his cheek. "Thanks, Julian."

"Did you get what you need?" Mama asked from the stove.

"Yes." I held the putty out for her to see. "But now I need popcorn."

"Dinner will be ready soon."

I walked over to the stove.

"It's for science."

Mama's left eyebrow raised, her lips pulled to one side.

"I'm serious," I said.

"Okay." She reached for the jar of kernels. "But you know how your father gets. If he gets feisty, I'm blaming you."

She put a pan on the stove to pop some corn for me.

I ran back to the garage and pinched the putty onto the axle. I plugged in a small fan and pointed it at my turbine. The cardboard blades shuddered and then spun, pulling the mermaid cups along the belt.

"Isabelle!" Mama called from the back door.

I ran inside and returned to the garage with a large bowl of popcorn. I slid it underneath the bottom bicycle tire. It took a few tries to get the correct height. I moved my bike an inch too far down and the cups hit the side of the bowl. I raised it too high and the cups brushed the top of the popcorn and returned empty. After half a dozen tries, it finally worked.

"What is this amazingness?" Papa asked, appearing like a

vision at the doorway to the garage, pulling his work apron over the top of his head.

"It's a wind-powered popcorn dispenser." I smiled. "Well, right now I'm using a fan for testing purposes. But, theoretically, it could be powered by the wind alone."

"Isabelle!" His eyes glittered as he stepped forward, as if in a trance. He watched the cup inch down the fabric belt, scoop up a few pieces of popcorn, lift them up to the top of the pulley, and drop them onto the table. "I don't think anything could make me happier."

"I knew I'd find you here." Mama's eyes were on Papa as his hands snuck the popcorn off the table. "It's almost time for dinner. Popcorn can wait."

Papa knew better than to frown, but he waited until Mama's eyes flashed toward the house, to where Julian sat inside the kitchen, before he slipped the popcorn into his mouth. Mama's eyes were quick, but so was Papa's chewing.

"Seven seizures," she said.

Papa froze mid-chew.

"What?" he asked.

"Julian's had seven seizures today. Each one less than ten seconds long."

"Inez," Papa said, stepping away from my turbine and wrapping his arms around my mother, "that is amazing."

Mama smiled. When she looked up at Papa, her eyes changed ever so slightly.

"How was he?"

Papa looked at me before responding to Mama. "Same as

always," he grumbled.

"He's still coming by on Thursday, for his birthday?"

"I'm assuming so," Papa said. "Restaurants are too crowded for him, and we can't bring Julian over to his house."

It had always been a problem, my grandfather's house not being accessible.

Mama's eyes spied popcorn caught in Papa's mustache. "Hernando, try to control yourself. I'm going in. I've got to keep an eye on Julian."

She slipped back inside, the kitchen door slamming behind her.

"What's going on?" I asked.

"I let Jimmy run the store for a few hours so I could swing by your grandfather's house." Papa scooped a fistful of popcorn into his mouth. "Your mother wanted me to check in on him, since we haven't seen him since before—"

"Before Julian's big seizure."

Papa nodded.

"And?" I asked.

"He's still as stubborn as ever."

Papa picked a kernel from a molar with his fingernail.

"He just seems grumpy to me."

"That, too. Do you mind if I have a bit more?" Papa asked, pointing to the growing pile of popcorn on the table. I nodded. "Your *abuelito* will be here for his birthday this week. Maybe if Julian's medication is working and your grandfather sees that the seizures are going away, he'll visit more often."

"He's still scared of the seizures?" I asked.

"It's not that he's scared. He . . . it's just hard for him, that's all."

"Papa, it's been fifteen years."

"I know." Papa nodded and offered me a smile. "Some people need more time than others."

"Isabelle, Hernando! Dinner's ready!" Mama called from the kitchen window.

"You go in first, Isabelle. I just need a minute."

Papa scooped up the bowl of popcorn, cradled it in his arms like a baby, and slipped behind the garage.

6

Later that night, I sat on Mama's chair, with my back against
Julian's bed and my hand holding his. The radiator whistled
and I waited to see a cloud of steam swoop in like a genie from
a magic lamp and lift us away. The wind smacked Julian's window and I expected the glass to burst so that Julian and I could
clamber out through the window frame and into Las Brisas.

I peeked under the bed. I craned my neck to see if there was
any movement or light coming from Julian's closet. I glanced at
the pinwheel and watched its steady spin.

And then I remembered.

It only happened when I relaxed. Julian had told me so
himself.

Taking a breath, I leaned against his bed and pressed my head
deep into his mattress. My hand gripped Julian's firmly, while
everything else loosened: my jaw dropped, my eyelids drooped,
my shoulders sagged, and my breathing grew heavy. Then, and
only then, did it happen.

As though someone was whispering into my ear, "Now, now,
NOW," my eyes snapped open. The mattress moved against my
head as Julian shifted his weight and sat up. Sliding his legs off
the edge, he looked down at me expectantly and clasped my hand.

"That sounds amazing," Julian began.

"What?" I whispered back.

"Your turbine project. When will you try it out?"

"I already did! Don't you remember?"

Julian's eyebrows bunched together.

"I told you at dinner."

"I don't remember that." Julian shook his head. "What did you make?"

"I put together a popcorn dispenser."

"I do remember the smell of popcorn," Julian said thoughtfully. "How'd you think of it?"

"I don't know," I said, remembering the hours spent sketching plans in my notebook, scrounging for supplies, and the shivers of excitement when everything came together.

We sat quietly and waited. Our breathing slowed. Our heartbeats slowed. The silence settled.

"Isabelle, look! The walls . . ." Julian whispered.

The wallpaper was slowly peeling off the walls. Underneath was a film as fragile as butterfly wings. The walls behind and the ceiling overhead vanished. Light glowed from beyond the textured, now tissue-paper-thin walls.

Julian stood, pulling me up with him. Reaching out, our fingertips pressed the paper. The wallpaper trembled and glittered. In one smooth ripple, it dropped like a curtain of golden dust, forming a shimmering ring around our feet.

Suddenly, we were standing side by side, together, in total darkness.

Even though Julian's room was dark, Las Brisas was darker.

"Where are we?" I whispered.

"I don't know," he said. He put both of his hands over mine for a moment to reassure me.

"Have you been here before?" I whispered.

"No—not that I can remember."

I felt the warmth of Julian standing beside me as a breeze crept up my back.

"Belle, do you smell what I smell?" he asked.

"What do you smell?" I sniffed, but noticed nothing—no scent, no sound, no movement.

"The ocean," Julian said. "It's very faint, but I smell seaweed, salt, and sand."

As he spoke, I was once again sucked into the melody of Julian's words. His voice was so beautiful and so strong, a voice like none I'd ever heard before. Julian spoke differently at home. He had a range of sounds and notes, cries and whispers. By the pitch of his voice we knew his mood. We could tell whether he was happy, frustrated, or tired, but he could never go into specifics. He couldn't explain himself. He couldn't describe.

Standing beside him in Las Brisas, I began to feel just how frustrating that must be.

My nose searched the air, the way Papa hunted down bags of microwave popcorn. And sure enough, I found it: The smell of the ocean pricked my nose as the landscape changed. Salt.

A horizon gradually appeared before us.

"Are we back at the cenote?" I asked.

"No, it's too cold," Julian said. "Come on, Belle, we should get moving."

Julian led the way. His eyes adjusted to Las Brisas faster than mine.

"Look, Belle. There's a light," he whispered.

I squinted and saw a beam of light swooping in front of us. As we neared, it illuminated a lighthouse, which reached high into the blackened sky. The beacon glowed an iridescent green with glints of turquoise, the color of the tail feathers on a quetzal.

"Should we go to it?" I asked.

"Why not?" Julian held my hand tighter. His grip was firm, like Papa's whenever we walked through crowded parking lots.

We climbed the stony hill. I stumbled a few times, but Julian kept me upright. His pace was quick; there was a drive about him.

At the base of the lighthouse, we waited in darkness for the light to return. We reached out and felt the cold, damp tower wall. When the light returned, Julian spied a door. He reached it first and turned the knob.

Inside, with shimmers of light pouring in from the narrow windows, we paused. A staircase snaked along the wall like a thick braid, twisting up and disappearing from view. For a moment, my stomach lurched, and I wondered how Julian could reach the top. Then I remembered: We weren't home. We were in Las Brisas. Julian could use his legs—and he never seemed to get tired.

Each step felt familiar: the way the railing cut into the wall and slid inside my palm, the way the steps grew brighter as we ascended. Piece by piece, it all came back to me.

"Julian, stop," I whispered, tugging on the hem of his pajama shirt.

"What is it?" He turned around, the light framing him from behind, his face hidden by shadow.

"I've been here before."

Julian turned and looked up, his profile revealed in the glow of the light. And ever so slightly, his expression changed.

"Are you sure, Belle?"

"I'm positive."

Julian's fingers traced the stone wall.

"I don't think I've ever visited a lighthouse," he said. "This must be the one you told me about, the one you and Tía Lucy visited last year during Tía Week."

I swallowed and stepped closer to him.

"I'm sorry you couldn't come with us that day," I said softly.

Tía Lucy called it Tía Week. Mama didn't disagree. Papa called it Summer Unvacation. Regardless of what it was called, Tía Lucy was my mother's older sister. She lived across the country in Los Angeles with my *tío* Santi, who was regionally famous for being Southern California's Taco King. Tío Santi was the founder of the popular Taco King restaurants and Taco King Puppy Boutiques.

Tía Lucy flew in every June for the first week of summer vacation with her two tamale-size Chihuahuas. She spent the first half of the week over at Abuelito's house. There, she cooked a month's worth of food and filled his freezer with single-serving packages of enchiladas and sweets, using the Taco King's secret recipes. When Abuelito's gruffness got the better of her, she arrived at our door with too many bags, more shoes than you could ever wear in a month, and a modified baby stroller for her dogs.

Tía Lucy's hair was jet black, except for streaks of silver just above her ears. On her left hand was a diamond so big it drooped and spun around on her finger. Her acrylic nails tick-tacked over anything they touched. Her lips were covered in bright red lipstick—until she spread the color across my cheeks and Julian's forehead.

As Papa always said: First she spreads the lipstick, then she spreads the advice.

Last year, Tía Lucy had barely placed her bottom on our couch before it all started.

"Inez, you aren't fluffing your pillows properly." She plucked a pillow off the couch. "Step away from the kids and come over here. Let me show you how it's done."

Tía Lucy smacked the pillow with her open palm and delicately placed it on the couch. It didn't strike me as particularly different, but Mama paused while cleaning Julian's feeding tube to step into the living room and fluff pillows. I took Mama's place at the kitchen sink and dipped the tube into a tub of warm, soapy water. I swished it around, just like I'd been taught, and then I rinsed it through. When I placed it on the drying rack, the tube coiled up like a drowsy rattle-snake. The pillow fluffing continued, so I wheeled Julian over to the kitchen table. We sat together, watching my mother fluff and arrange pillows for much longer than was necessary. Papa took five trips up and down the stairs, lugging Tía's suitcases up to my bedroom.

"Well, I have to admit that they look lovely," my mother said as she sat down on the couch and gingerly leaned against the fluffed pillows. Tía Lucy smiled and pulled her Chihuahuas out from her purse. They hopped on the couch and snuggled in beside her. Mama leaned over and scratched their heads.

"Oh, Inez," Tía Lucy said, shaking her head. "That is not the way to scratch a Chihuahua."

Tía Lucy scooped up the tiniest of her Chihuahuas, Sanchita, and held her close to my mother. "You have to rub under Sanchita's chin while you scratch from the tip of her ear."

"Ahem," Papa interrupted, standing at the base of the stairs. "Their ears are one inch long—how much is there to scratch?"

"One inch," Tía Lucy clarified. Sanchita's eyes pinched closed. Her thin lips turned up in a doggie smile.

"Lucia," Mama said, passing the tiny dog back to her sister, "her teeth are chattering."

"Oh dear." Tía Lucy clutched the dog, ran to her doggie stroller, and pulled out something fuzzy. "The girls aren't used to this New England weather."

Once Sanchita was cozy in a doll-size sweater and subdued with proper ear scratches, Tía Lucy carefully lifted Big Betty and placed the pudgy Chihuahua on my mother's lap.

"Big Betty has her own ear-scratching preference." Tía Lucy locked eyes with Papa. "And don't give me that look, Hernando. You might think that sister Chihuahuas like their ears scratched the same way, but you would be mistaken."

Papa walked over to the table and leaned close to my ear.

"Isabelle, why don't you leave the Taco Queen and take Julian to his room," Papa suggested.

"Aye, Hernando, you know I don't like you calling me the Taco Queen," Tía Lucy shouted from the living room.

I wheeled Julian into his room as my mother learned Big Betty's counterclockwise ear-scratch technique.

I pulled Julian's red plastic ball out from his toy basket and slipped it into his hand. He squeezed it in his fist, strengthening his finger muscles. I saw the tendons tighten and his knuckles turn white. Once he grew tired of the red ball, I moved on to a different therapy toy.

"While they are nice and relaxed, let me show you Sanchita's new sweater collection," Tía Lucy's voice rang out.

It wasn't long before Papa's head poked into Julian's room. He was pulling at the collar of his shirt.

"There's only so much of the Taco Queen I can take," he grumbled.

"Hernando!" Tía Lucy shouted.

Papa smiled as he stepped inside.

"I'm going for a jog. Keep your brother company, okay?"

"I was going to anyway," I said.

Julian and I played a game of Memory and listened to some music. We painted with watercolors, Julian practicing his swirls as I painted portraits of Sanchita and Big Betty. We finished just as an eight-second seizure interrupted Julian's painting. His brush toppled out of his grip, bounced off his tray, and landed on the floor. I comforted him, wiped up the mess, and recorded the seizure.

Later, I wheeled Julian into the backyard where we held pinwheels against the wind. I blew bubbles and he watched them float into the sky.

Soon it was time to hook up Julian's feeding tube and start his next feed. Mama waved us inside.

"I've mixed it all up; I just need you to attach the tube." She rubbed my back. "Thank you, Isabelle."

In the kitchen, Mama seasoned the Taco King's famous tacos. The recipe was trademarked and extremely time-intensive. Mama and Tía Lucy roasted chilies and ground them in a *molcajete* before rolling out the tortillas by hand.

Papa returned, sweaty and smelly, just in time for dinner.

Once we were all seated, our tortillas sufficiently stuffed, the Chihuahuas safely snoozing in their doggie stroller, Tía Lucy tapped her glass with her fork.

"This visit has only just begun, and already, I've loved every minute," Tía Lucy announced.

Papa's mustache twitched. His eyes were on his tacos. The table vibrated and the Chihuahuas started barking.

"You'll have to excuse Hernando's stomach," Mama apologized. "Long jogs make him hungry."

"Oh, please eat!" Tía Lucy exclaimed. Papa shoved the first taco in his mouth and ate it whole. Tía Lucy nodded in admiration. "Every year, I come all the way from Los Angeles to spend time with you."

"We're always happy to have you," Mama said.

Papa kept his head tucked as he popped his second taco in his mouth.

"Almost all of you." Tía Lucy smiled and took a deep breath. "And so, I feel it is my duty to state an important observation. I have noticed that Isabelle isn't getting enough attention. Every time I look around, she's taking care of her brother. She needs time for herself."

Tía Lucy took a dainty bite of her taco and delicately patted her mouth with a napkin.

"I don't think Isabelle's deprived of attention." Mama turned to me, searching for affirmation. I took a bite of taco.

Tía Lucy arched one of her penciled-on eyebrows.

"Inez, didn't you notice that Isabelle cared for her brother all day? She helped him with his physical therapy. She played with his wing-dings outside." Tía Lucy took another bite of her taco and savored it for a moment. "She also got his medications ready. She set up his feeding machine. Oh, I could go on and on. It is quite clear that young Isabelle is too preoccupied by her brother, and it's not okay."

"Lucia, you preoccupied Inez with your frivolous and ridiculous—ow!" Papa stooped over and rubbed his leg. Mama closed her eyes and sighed deeply while Papa arranged six more tacos on his plate.

My mother's forehead wrinkled, and my father frowned.

Tía Lucy broke the silence.

"I've decided to take Isabelle for the day tomorrow—a girls' day out."

Her nails drummed a rhythm on the tabletop. She smiled broadly and turned to look at me.

"We'll take the babies and go exploring. You won't have to worry about helping out. You won't have to think about Julian or his seizures for a whole day. How does that sound?"

"You're leaving us for the day?" Papa's smile was a little too big. "And you're taking your babies—I mean, dogs?"

"Because of Julian?" I asked, but Tía Lucy didn't hear me. She was already telling a story about the time Sanchita and Big Betty had snuck into her purse before she'd left for the cinema. During the scariest part of the zombie movie, the Chihuahuas hopped out of her purse and nipped at the heels of the moviegoers, sending the entire cinema into hysterics. Tía Lucy laughed at the memory.

"Sadly, we are now forbidden from that theater," Tía Lucy concluded woefully, shaking her head.

Dinner dragged on. Papa ate too many tacos; Tía Lucy told too many Chihuahua stories. Julian had a tiny seizure while Mama praised Tía Lucy's Taco King Tart.

When the meal was finished, Mama followed me up to my room and helped me set up my sleeping bag.

"Did Tía Lucy tell you where we're going tomorrow?" I asked.

"No, it's a secret. I didn't even know she was planning it," Mama began, unrolling my sleeping bag and smoothing it out with her palms.

"She surprised me, too," I said, laying my pillow down.

"Isabelle . . . "

"Yes, Mama?"

She pulled the zipper open and looked over at me. Doubt and worry created wrinkles around her eyes.

"Never mind." Mama kissed me on the forehead. "Get some rest."

I slipped into my sleeping bag while Mama turned off the

lights. When she reached the door, she hesitated.

"Isabelle, you'd tell me if you felt overlooked. If you felt we asked too much of you. Right?"

I nodded.

"You promise?" she asked.

"Promise," I said. Mama nodded, more to herself than to me, and then shut the door carefully behind her.

The next morning, Tía Lucy met me at the bottom of the steps, a cooler in one hand, a Maine guidebook in the other.

"Ready for our road trip?" she called out. She wore a string of pearls, and her perfume rose up around her like a cloud of floral exhaust. "I packed breakfast and lunch."

Mama was still in her pajamas as she prepared Julian's meds. Papa sat at the table filling a mixing bowl with cereal and milk. I didn't think it was possible, but his smile looked even larger than the night before.

"Hurry up, Isabelle. The Taco Queen is ready to go." He chuckled.

Tía Lucy frowned only momentarily.

"I'm ready," I said, slipping my shoes on.

Tía Lucy adjusted her hair in the mirror before turning back to me.

"I don't want you worrying about seizures, or tubes, or medicines, or anything today. You need to be free to have fun. You deserve a day that is just for you, Isabelle."

Mama said nothing and continued sorting Julian's meds. Papa's smile faded a little. And then he stood, placed a hand on Julian's shoulder, and cleared his throat.

"Isabelle, think of today as an adventure. It's not every day you get to go on a road trip with a Taco Queen and her two pet rats."

"Rats! I'll have you know that my Chihuahuas come from prize-winning parents, even though Big Betty's belly is a bit outside the typical pedigree norms."

Papa didn't say anything else, but instead, wheeled Julian over to the back door so he could look outside at his wind toys.

"What if Julian wants to come?" I asked.

Tía Lucy handed me my jacket. "Don't worry, Belle. He won't even know that you're gone," she said.

I pulled away.

"Of course he will. Julian knows when I'm around." I zipped my coat. "And please don't call me Belle. I only want Julian to call me that."

Tía Lucy pulled back. "What?"

"If . . . if he could talk, I would want him to call me Belle." My cheeks felt warm.

"She's so neglected that she's developed an overstimulated imagination, too," Tía Lucy said. She bit her lip and looked over at my mother.

"There's nothing wrong with pretending," Mama said.

Before we left, I pulled Julian's favorite toy from his bin— the hand-carved maraca Papa had bought in Oaxaca years ago. I brought it over to Julian and placed his fingers on the carvings. He followed them around the bulb until his hand slipped down to the handle. The sound of dried beans filled my ears. Julian could play that maraca for hours.

Reluctantly, I followed Tía Lucy out of the house and buck-led myself into her rental car.

I munched a bagel as we rode along the empty highway. Sanchita and Big Betty sat on Tía Lucy's shoulders like parrots. They wore matching leopard-print sweaters and only shivered out of habit. We eventually turned onto a side road. Out the window, I saw waves of long grass wrapped around inlets of salt water. A blue heron turned to watch our car drive past. Soon, the grass gave way to rocks and sand as the ocean came into view.

"How old are Sanchita and Big Betty?" I asked, breaking the silence in the car. The Chihuahuas turned their tiny, pointed noses in my direction.

"Three years, four weeks, and one day old," Tía Lucy replied.

I had forgotten that Tía Lucy also shared my mother's magic memory. They were so different in so many ways, it was easy to forget they shared this special gift.

Eventually, Tía Lucy pulled into a gravel parking lot. Off in the distance stood a lighthouse.

"Isn't that a sight?" she exclaimed. "Come on, Isabelle, let's explore."

Tía Lucy delicately stepped from her car and went to the trunk. She unfolded her dog stroller in one smooth motion. Sanchita and Big Betty hopped down from their perch and curled up inside. As we walked up the path to the lighthouse, more than a few people stopped to stare. It wasn't every day you saw a woman marching up a hill wearing red high-heeled sandals and pushing a doggie stroller.

The lighthouse sat at the end of a long peninsula, with cliffs on either side. The wind whipped and tugged at my jacket. My hands balled up in my pockets as we reached the top of the hill.

"My, my, my. This is so beautiful," Tía Lucy declared, gazing up at the lighthouse.

Families streamed in and out of the small wooden door. Dads paused to take photos with cameras slung around their necks; moms reminded their children to keep away from the bluff's edges. Tía Lucy parked her stroller beside the lighthouse and nestled her dogs inside her purse.

Once we stepped inside the doorway, everything felt different. The air was no longer warm with sunshine. The space was raw and clammy. Light squeezed through the narrow windows. Sanchita and Big Betty trembled.

Trudging up the steps behind Tía Lucy, my thighs burned. The *tap, tap, tap* of her shoes kept up a steady rhythm, never missing a beat.

I paused and looked up. The staircase twisted like Julian's feeding tubes. My arm brushed against the stone wall. I scooted over as an elderly man with a cane inched his way down. I frowned. The staircase was too narrow and too long. There was no way Papa could carry Julian to the top. I shook my head and pushed the thought away.

We stepped out of the stairwell and onto the landing. It was like walking out of an underground dungeon and into Oz. There wasn't a cloud in the sky and the ocean poured out before us. Thundering waves slapped the stones below. Gulls swooped, trying to catch the rising white caps before they fell.

"*¡Que linda!*" Tía Lucy said. She wrapped her arms around

my shoulders and squeezed me tight.

"Yes, it *is* so beautiful!" I exclaimed as I took a deep breath. The wind blew my hair around my face, and for a few seconds, I felt it lifting me up.

Tía Lucy pulled a small digital camera out from her purse, where it had nestled between Sanchita and Big Betty.

I posed against the railing and smiled.

"You have such a lovely smile—it looks so much like mine!" she said, pulling me in for a hug. "Now, isn't this a great way to spend the day?"

"It sure is," I said, and her arms tightened around me.

"I'm sure anything beats sitting at home playing nurse for your brother."

I wiggled my shoulders and drew her arms back. Her hug suddenly felt stifling—like too many scarves wrapped around my neck on a March afternoon.

"I don't *play* nurse," I said.

Tía Lucy looked down at me. Her skin glowed, dark and rich from the California sunshine.

"You're right. Isabelle, you help out too much for it to be considered playing. Julian is a lot of work. You can't let his seizures hold you down. Just because he's disabled and can't do anything doesn't mean you need to suffer, too."

I blinked my eyes a few times and rubbed the wind out of my ears. When I found my voice, the words tumbled out.

"That's not true. He's *not* disabled. He just can't do certain things."

"It is true, Isabelle. Your mother spends her whole day

tracking and counting, and so do you." She took a deep breath and stooped close to me. "I brought you here so you could have a fun day just for you. Would Julian be able to experience all this? No. No, he wouldn't."

"That's not true," I said again, my voice louder.

I shivered even in the warmth of the sun. Standing at the top of the lighthouse no longer felt magnificent. The piercing wind and the smell of the ocean blowing in from lands so far away made me feel alone. Sanchita and Big Betty peered up at me, their dark brown eyes watering in the wind.

"Just because Julian has seizures, that doesn't mean he can't do things. If he was here, he'd love to smell the salt air, he'd—"

"Julian can't climb the steps," Tía Lucy pointed out as she brushed hair out of her eyes.

"It's not just about the stairs," I said.

"Of course it's not just about the stairs." Tía Lucy's voice was growing impatient. Her words were crisp and sharp and a little too loud. "If Julian were here, you'd be worrying about his seizures. You wouldn't have climbed up those steps. You wouldn't be looking at this incredible view." Sanchita and Big Betty ducked inside the purse until only their noses were visible. "Our time together would be interrupted."

I thought about the twisty, uneven, spiral steps. I looked past Tía Lucy, to the water stretching out into the distance, waves over waves melting into a haze of blue.

"Well, you're right. If Julian were here, I might have stayed down at the bottom." As I spoke, from the corner of my eye I saw Tía Lucy nodding. I looked at her and continued. "But maybe

I would have climbed up and taken photos to share with him."

Tía Lucy still looked doubtful. She tapped her foot impatiently.

"Yes, I suppose." Big Betty and Sanchita swung their front paws over the top of Tía Lucy's bag. Their eyes squinted and their long eyelashes blew in the wind. Tía Lucy cleared her throat. "Come, the girls are hungry. Let's eat."

We wound our way down the steps and pushed the dogs back to the car in the stroller. Tía Lucy pulled a blanket out from the trunk. I carried the cooler.

"Peek inside, Isabelle. I made your favorite torta," she said with a wink.

I unzipped the cooler and pulled out a sandwich carefully wrapped in wax paper.

"With avocado and pineapple?" I asked.

"Just the way you like it." My stomach rumbled like Papa's.

I helped Tía Lucy spread the blanket on a hillside. While Tía Lucy ate fruit salad with a toothpick and hand-fed her Chihuahuas bite-size strips of boiled chicken, I devoured my torta and picked buttercups. As I picked, I thought of all the birthday parties and playdates I'd been to, surrounded by friends and, often, their brothers and sisters. Julian was never able to join me. Maybe it was because Mama wanted to give me some *me* time, like Tía Lucy said: time to play with my friends and not worry about Julian's seizures. Maybe Julian never came because my friends' houses weren't accessible. They had too many steps leading up from their driveway, or their doorways were too narrow. Maybe he just wasn't invited, plain and simple.

Julian couldn't eat cake or tell funny jokes, but he could

swing a bat at a piñata, he could help blow out candles, and he always smiled when he heard laughter. I guess my friends didn't know that. Maybe my aunt didn't know it either.

I pulled my hair elastic off the tip of my braid and wrapped it around the stems on my buttercup bouquet.

"There," I said, with satisfaction.

The crisp air blew across the long sea grass, brushing against my toes and my legs. I wondered if the breeze felt the same to Julian, if it felt as soft against his skin and sent goose bumps up to his shoulders. Big Betty snuggled in beside me and Sanchita sniffed at my buttercups.

"Tía Lucy . . ." I began.

"Sí?" She turned and focused the camera on me and her dogs.

"Papa used to carry Julian out into the woods when we chopped down our Christmas tree—his wheelchair isn't too good in the woods. When Julian got too big, I had Mama buy a special sled, so we could continue the tradition.

"Sometimes the best trees are tough to get to. Julian's sled can't fit, or the ground is too bumpy, or there's not enough snow on the ground. So, I go on ahead and Papa cuts off a branch for me. I bring it back to Julian. Julian smells the pine needles and feels how sharp they are. I tell him how the tree looks—how tall it is, and what shape. Julian gives me a thumbs-down if he wants to keep looking. We usually spend an hour searching for the perfect tree. When we find it, Julian gives me a thumbs-up."

Tía Lucy's camera slipped down, away from her face. She stepped closer, her eyes scanning the ocean.

"And then what happens?" she asked.

"If Julian can't be next to the tree when Mama and Papa cut it down, I tell him what I see. He can hear the saw. He can smell the pine. He can feel the December air. Once it's cut, Mama and Papa lay it on his sled and then we pull Julian and the tree back to the car."

Tía Lucy flicked off her shoes and sat down beside me.

I looked at her closely. "Maybe next year, Julian can come here with us."

"Would you have enjoyed this more if Julian had come?" Her voice didn't question the way her words did.

"Yes," I said. "It's not just that Julian isn't here; it's that you didn't even invite him. There are so many things that Julian can't do, like climb up those steps. But—"

"I get it, Isabelle."

"You do?"

"Yes, I think so. If Julian were here, he'd be enjoying this hill with us right now," Tía Lucy said, as she simultaneously scratched Sanchita's and Big Betty's ears. Both dogs looked unhappy, as their preferred style of ear scratching involved two hands. I grabbed Big Betty and began her counterclockwise scratching.

"So . . . we'll come back again next year with Julian, Taco Queen?" I asked.

"Only if you promise to never call me that again," she said with a grin.

But all that was last year, before Julian's big seizure. Now, tonight, in Las Brisas, there was no ocean view when Julian and I reached the top of the lighthouse—just ever-expanding darkness that swirled and lapped at the sides of the tower like tongues of smoke. The sky was empty of stars. A film of black clouds masked the moon.

Julian leaned into me. "There's no view," he whispered.

"Maybe because you'll be coming with me and Tía Lucy this year."

"But, Isabelle," he said, pausing, "I'll never make it to the top."

My throat burned and my eyes stung. "You can still feel the ocean breeze on the hill." I put my hand on his. "You can feel the buttercups, hear the waves, and smell the salt air. Maybe I can take Papa's phone to the top and you can have Mama's on the bottom, and we can do a video chat so you can see what I see."

Julian's eyes filled with longing as he stared out into the distance. His face grew serious and thoughtful, with furrowed brows and a strained smile.

"What is it?" I asked.

Julian blinked away some tears as his hands gripped the railing. His knuckles turned white.

"Julian . . ."

"Tía Lucy was right, you know."

"What are you talking about?" I moved in closer.

"When you stay home and watch me, you aren't doing something for yourself. I don't want to hold you back."

"I make my own choices, Julian."

"I don't want to hold you back," he repeated.

In a heartbeat, I was back in Julian's room leaning against

his mattress. Our hands were nearly stuck together with sweat. His breathing was deep. I straightened my stiff knees and took a few staggering steps.

Soft morning light poured into Julian's room. The sun peeked through the leaves, casting an orange glow on the new morning. It felt like we'd only been in Las Brisas for a short time, but I could hear Mama's footsteps heading down the stairs.

Each Tuesday when Mrs. Pemberly came and made music with Julian, his eyes caught fire. He emerged like a cicada from beneath the earth, fresh and new, shiny, wriggling, and alive. Her voice ached with beauty. Her high notes were like marionette strings lifting Julian's spirits up to the clouds. The deep notes rumbled inside his body, like the hum of tectonic plates.

Mrs. Pemberly wore frilly, tiered skirts and thick-strapped sandals—even in the winter. Her toenails were painted in rainbow colors; her hair was a mess of black and gray corkscrew curls. She wore bracelets that clinked and clanked and sometimes slid off her wrists. She spoke with the loudest voice I'd ever heard— louder than Papa when he had the hiccups, and louder than our principal on the speaker that time the eighth-grade toilets got backed up with milk cartons.

To me, Mrs. Pemberly wasn't just a musician; she was a fairy godmother—Julian's fairy godmother. Her wand was her voice, her guitar, her tambourine, her presence. She made the walls in our house tremble. She made the lines of worry disappear from Mama's face. Like the Pied Piper, once a week her music stole Julian's seizures away, luring them to another world.

Each week, Mrs. Pemberly sat next to Julian or propped him up beside her and sang her ridiculous songs—about a bullfrog wearing a cowboy hat, or an old brown cow with a mustache (or, as she would sing it, a *moostache*), or the circus train clickity-clacking down the winding rails, off to fetch some pineapples. The lyrics were goofy and the songs were loud. The students in my chorus class would have rolled their eyes or laughed until their bellies ached.

But not me.

I craved those songs. I yearned for those songs. And that Tuesday, with Julian slouching in his wheelchair, breathing deep, sleepy breaths, I needed those songs.

"The buh-buh-buh-bullfrog jumped . . ." Mrs. Pemberly bounded from the floor, her hair springing, her bracelets jangling. When she landed again, she shook Julian's hand and the tambourine drizzled its chimes into the room.

". . . and landed on a tin roof."

Julian's eyes stayed closed, but he lifted his arm. The tambourine slid out of his grasp and clanked onto his tray.

"Hold on!" Mrs. Pemberly threw her arms up, stopping all music and breath. Pressing the tambourine back in his hand, she gave him a few practice shakes. "Julian, Julian, my dear, sweet boy. You've got to hold on tight! You have to fight off this sleep. You can do this. Feel the tambourine. Become one with it. Let's do that line again!"

Julian's eyes opened and met hers. It took great effort, but he smiled, and Mrs. Pemberly strummed her guitar in response.

"The buh-buh-buh-bullfrog jumped . . ." we sang again.

Julian's hand clasped tighter and shook the tambourine, all on his own. He held it high and perfectly, rhythmically, matched the tapping of Mrs. Pemberly's feet.

". . . and landed on a tin roof!"

Julian shook the tambourine fiercely this time. I picked up his maraca and joined in.

"The roof was hoh-hoh-hoh-hot. The frog went splat!"

Mrs. Pemberly pounded on her bongo. Mama and I jumped out of our seats. Julian sat, eyes opened wide, a smile on his face.

"Let's repeat the verse, Julian, let's repeat!"

Mrs. Pemberly and I sang the ridiculous song about the bull-frog landing on a hot tin roof and frying itself crisp, over and over and over again. It was a never-ending circle of fried frogs, with Julian's tambourine matching the beat.

"Well done, Julian! Bravo! Bravo!" Mrs. Pemberly gave him a round of applause when we'd finished. She stood up and bowed down to him, before turning to my mother.

"Now, Inez," Mrs. Pemberly said, attaching a strip of jingle bells around Julian's wrist as his eyes slipped closed.

Mama inched forward. "Yes?"

"I've been thinking of putting together a small orchestra made up of a few of my highest-achieving musical students."

Mama and I both waited for Mrs. Pemberly to go on. She was the type of talker who took deep pauses in the middle of her thoughts. She fluffed her curls and tuned her guitar. Julian's eyes pinched closed.

She continued, "I would be honored to have Julian take part."

"You want Julian to be in an orchestra?" Mama asked. She didn't hide the shock in her voice.

"Why, yes, I do." Mrs. Pemberly batted her long lashes at my mother, her eyes wide.

"What instrument will he play?" I asked.

"I've given it some thought." Mrs. Pemberly smoothed her skirt, adjusted her bangles, and re-fluffed her curls. "Though I know he is quite fond of his maraca, Julian is a master at the tambourine." She paused again, this time cradling Julian's maraca against her bosom. She delicately placed it in Julian's basket of musical instruments. "I see so much potential with this instrument. Oh, how I love the ringing of a well-played tambourine! Julian would be joining two other students: Sylvia, who excels at the bongo, and Dylan, who is learning the recorder. I believe Dylan and Julian have an art class together."

Mrs. Pemberly reached out and shook Julian's wrists. Julian's arms were limp in her hands and his chin was tucked into his neck. She shook them again. The tambourine rang out with its crisp, clean notes.

Julian's eyes opened, but his gaze was focused on the floor.

"Julian," Mrs. Pemberly said, scooting closer, her lips now inches from Julian's left ear, "let's give these jingle bells another try. You jazzed them up so well last time. Come on, Julian. You can do it."

She pulled her guitar over her head and started strumming. For a moment, I was lost in the notes. Her fingers raced over the guitar strings with such speed and force that my eyes couldn't keep up. Too soon, and too suddenly, she stopped.

Julian's eyes had closed.

"Julian. Julian, my sweet boy—" Mrs. Pemberly leaned forward again. She massaged his hands in hers, and then began tapping his wrist. "The beat is one-two-three-pause, one-two-three-pause. Feel it in your gut, your breath. Feel it in your being." She shook his wrist a few times to set the rhythm. It took a dozen tries, but finally, Julian's eyes were open and focused.

Mrs. Pemberly sang a new song about chirping birds sitting on a fence, arguing about who had the fluffiest feathers. Julian kept the beat pretty well. Every now and again, his eyes closed. Each time, Mrs. Pemberly gently clasped his wrist to guide him farther. I found myself wondering if this orchestra would be made up of kids each playing to their own rhythm, or if they'd fall into a shared one naturally.

By the end of the song, Julian was alert, and with Mrs. Pemberly's guidance, his rhythm was spot on. My heart swelled.

"I know we usually meet on Tuesdays, Inez," Mrs. Pemberly said as she packed up her gear, "but would it be okay if we also meet on Thursdays, for an additional orchestra session?"

Mama nodded and stood up.

Mrs. Pemberly shook her bangles and continued, "It would be at the same time, of course, starting next week. I'll have the lessons at my house. No worries—it's accessible."

"Next week on Wednesday; I'll mark the calendar," Mama said.

"No, no, dear," Mrs. Pemberly corrected, delicately placing her hand on my mother's shoulder. "I said Thursday."

Mama nodded again and walked to the calendar, where she paused and rubbed her forehead with her hands.

Mrs. Pemberly took no notice and sat down beside Julian.

"Julian, you did well with the jingle bells, but I'm going to have you stick with the tambourine. You've practiced with it far longer. This may not be the best time to try new things." She removed the bells from his wrists and placed the tambourine back on Julian's tray. "Wake up, my sweet boy," she said, squatting next to Julian's chair.

His breathing grew deep and his eyelashes settled on his cheeks. Julian wasn't going to wake up anytime soon, so I stepped forward.

"Mrs. Pemberly, give me the music. I'll show Julian when he wakes up. I'll help him practice."

She nodded. "Be sure he practices every day."

"I will."

I held the blue folder tight against my chest as Mama handed Mrs. Pemberly her check. I carried Mrs. Pemberly's percussion box to her beat-up station wagon. With her guitar and bongo, her long skirts and her bracelets, she needed the help.

"Is this your first orchestra?" I asked as I slid the box into her trunk.

"Oh, goodness no. I have one every couple of years." She lifted her guitar and tucked it beside the box. "It takes a careful combination of musicians to get an orchestra to play right."

"Do the other musicians have seizures?" I asked.

"No." She paused and looked up at the trees, thinking. "They are all gifted musicians. But you're not asking that. You want to know if they're like Julian."

I blushed.

"It's nothing to be embarrassed about. Dylan has a rather complex case of cerebral palsy; Sylvia is visually impaired."

I nodded and stuffed my hands in my pockets.

"Will they like Julian?" I asked.

"Of course." She looked at me with surprise. "What's not to like about him?"

I shrugged and slammed her trunk closed.

Maybe because I was lingering, or because she took frequent pauses, Mrs. Pemberly hesitated and looked at me.

"I like the way you talk to Julian," I blurted out.

"How do I talk to him?" Mrs. Pemberly stared at me with her round brown eyes.

I thought about it for a minute until I found the right words.

"You talk to him the same way you talk to me. Not everyone does."

"Well, Isabelle," she said, adjusting her bangles and leaning on her car door, "I like the way *you* are with Julian. There's love radiating all around you."

"Thanks." I smiled.

Mrs. Pemberly stooped down and put her hands on my shoulders. Her hands were strong and warm and smelled like mint.

"You believe in Julian, more than anyone else. He loves you for that."

"Mama and Papa believe in him," I said.

"They do." Mrs. Pemberly turned, opened her car door, and scooted into her seat. She pulled on her oversize sunglasses, and slammed the door shut. When her car started up, it buzzed like a garbage disposal filled with forks.

Mrs. Pemberly was halfway down the driveway when she stopped, poked her head out her open window, and waved me over. "Isabelle, your parents are also afraid."

"Afraid?" I asked.

"But you're not. That's why you're so important to him. You love without fear. You see possibilities."

With that, she turned her radio on full blast, pulled out of the driveway, and drove away.

"Julian," I called out, "let's try this one."

I walked over to Julian and placed his arm across the tray, leaving his hand dangling at the wrist. I positioned his chair a few inches from my bicycle turbine.

"Are you ready?" I asked.

Even though Julian's eyes were open, his muscle tone was weak. I leaned in closer. His eyes didn't find mine. They were turned down, and his eyelids began to close.

"Julian, it's the middle of the afternoon. It's not bedtime yet." I gave his shoulder a gentle shake. In response, he blinked, opened his eyes, and smiled.

Julian's love of the wind was not only the inspiration for my science fair project, he was also my assistant. He always listened as I presented new ideas. He never judged my scientific failures. He held anything I asked him to hold, so long as it was a reasonable size and less than five pounds.

And then Julian had had his most recent big seizure, and he'd been hospitalized. Now, with the science fair just days away and my new projects taking shape, our practice time was crucial. I slipped a new belt onto the bike tires. This one had small paintbrushes attached. For the practice round, a tray of water rested below. I switched on the fan and the turbine blades started to spin.

The first brush that swept across Julian's fingers was dry. His eyes widened with surprise. The belt pulled it up and the next brush skimmed the surface of the water. Drops fell to the ground as the brush traveled to Julian's waiting hand. When the cold bristles kissed his fingertips, Julian pulled his hand back.

"It's okay—it's just water," I explained. Julian's eyes found mine, to check the truth behind my words. I nodded, and his hand inched back over to the same spot, just as the next brush approached.

"Haven't you practiced enough?" Papa asked as he stepped into the garage, slipping his work apron over his head.

"There's no such thing as too much practice," I replied. "Watch this, Papa."

I pointed to the brushes. Julian's fingers flexed in anticipation of the next stroke of the brush. With each touch, his smile brightened.

"I'm impressed," Papa said.

"For my real presentation, I'll use paint. Right now, Julian and I just want to make sure everything's perfect. Right, Julian?"

His chin dipped, and his eyes started to close.

Papa's eyes darted between Julian and me as he pulled his jacket on carefully, holding his breath until the zipper had passed his belly. An orange poked out of an overstuffed jacket pocket, and the other one bulged strangely.

"What's Julian got to do with this?" Papa asked.

"I've told you, lots of times."

"Told me what?" Papa looked at Julian and then back at me. His mustache twitched.

"Julian's helping me during my presentation," I said, turning to Julian.

He snored softly in response.

"I don't remember you telling me about this. I must have forgotten."

I closed my eyes and bit the sides of my tongue to challenge the tears burning behind my eyelids.

"What is it, Isabelle?" Papa's voice was softer. I opened my eyes but kept them focused on my sneakers.

"Nothing," I muttered.

"It's not nothing." Papa brushed my cheek with a callused finger.

"I don't think you forgot. I just think that sometimes you don't hear me because . . ." I looked up to see Papa glancing at Julian yet again.

"Oh, Isabelle, I'm always listening. It's just that sometimes your mother and I—"

"I know, Papa. I know."

"Isabelle." Papa's voice was soft, dangerously soft. He took a deep breath and ran his hand through his hair. "Have you told your mother about this? She hasn't said anything to me. We'll need to coordinate with Julian's school."

"I told both of you," I said. As I looked away, my eyes caught sight of his jacket pocket. "You're taking the pickles?"

Papa's guilty look spread across his face.

I toweled off Julian's hand. Without looking at Papa, I continued.

"Mrs. Harris said that brothers and sisters can come to the science fair. Julian is the whole reason I've been studying wind. He helped me map the windiest places in the world." I peeked at Papa from the corner of my eye. "And besides, you've seen us researching for weeks."

"Isabelle," Papa said, taking one of his deep breaths as he peeled an orange. "Julian doesn't go to your school. I think Mrs. Harris meant that siblings who go to your school can come. Besides, your mother is carefully tracking Julian's seizures right now, because of his new medication."

"Of course she is."

"Isabelle, I don't like your tone."

I didn't like his tone, so I kept my mouth shut. Heavy silence hung between us.

"We are at a new stage with Julian, with his medicine and his seizures," Papa said. "It's probably not the best time to change his routine."

Papa handed me an orange wedge. He placed his hand on top of Julian's head and gently stroked his hair. He turned back to me and winced when he saw the disappointment on my face.

"Julian wants to come," I said quietly.

Papa reached for his backpack. Two jalapeños and three cheese sticks fell out of the front pocket. He snatched them up and shoved them back inside.

"Isabelle . . ." Papa looked over at Julian.

"It's true, Papa. Julian wants to come." I placed my hand on

Julian's arm and shook it gently. "Isn't that right, Julian?"

Papa looked at Julian.

"Julian," I said softly. "Julian . . ." I leaned in and pleaded into his ear. Julian's hand slowly reached out to mine, and I held it. His right eye opened and he fought to open his left. Papa popped both jalapeños into his mouth. I couldn't tell if his eyes were watering from tears, or from the spicy peppers.

"When is it?" Papa finally asked.

"Friday."

He cleared his throat.

"I'll talk to your mom."

I cheered and squeezed Julian's hand. "Did you hear that?" I asked.

Julian squeezed back in response.

Papa wrapped his arms around us. I closed my eyes and leaned into him. I felt the warmth of his hug despite the cold jar of pickles pressing into my ribs. And then a question popped into my head.

"How old was Julian when the seizures started?"

Julian's hand flexed inside mine. His other hand moved slowly across his tray.

"Well . . ." Papa looked at his watch, reached for a recycling bin, flipped it over, and sat down. "I guess they started right after he was born. But we didn't know that they were seizures until he was almost six months old."

"What do you mean?" I asked.

"Well, they started as small twitches, like he was waking himself up as he was falling asleep."

I looked at Papa. The crinkles around his eyes grew deeper. He split open a cheese stick, unscrewed the lid from the jar of pickles, dipped the cheese stick in the pickle juice, and then ate it whole.

"We finally realized something was wrong at a checkup, when his doctor noticed that Julian wasn't doing the typical things he should've been doing by that time."

"Oh."

"Finding out that Julian was having seizures was really hard, Isabelle. But once we knew, we realized we could help him get better."

Papa kissed Julian on his cheek as he stood up.

"Were you and Mama afraid that I might have seizures, too?" I asked.

"A little, but Julian's type of seizures are so rare, the chances of it happening twice in one family isn't likely. We also knew that if you had seizures like Julian, we'd love you, just as we love Julian."

Papa brought the jar of pickles to his mouth, took a gulp of pickle juice, and smiled.

"I'll never forget the moment I saw your chubby Perez cheeks and your beautiful brown eyes the day you were born. I didn't know what lay ahead, but I knew that you completed our family."

8

"Stand back."

Julian caught the seriousness in my voice and moved to the other side of the corridor. I twisted my lock, carefully entering the combination. I leaned my hip against the door, lifted the latch, and allowed the door to spring open.

Notebooks, highlighters, gym socks, sweatshirts, a hairbrush, and sheets of paper spilled out across the floor.

"Does this always happen?" Julian asked.

"No." I smiled. "Usually, I stand by the door and stop the avalanche, but I wanted you to get the full effect."

Julian stooped and gathered up my notebooks. I collected the highlighters and crammed them into a pencil case.

"I'm not touching those," Julian said, pointing his chin at my socks. "How many pairs?"

"I don't know. Six? I meant to take them home weeks ago, but, you know, I just haven't."

"It's the same under your bed."

"You've never seen under my bed." I paused and considered the power of Las Brisas. "Wait, *have* you seen under my bed?"

"No," Julian laughed. "But I've heard Mama and Papa complain about it."

Julian tucked my notebooks under some worn-out textbooks

on my locker shelf as I balled up my socks. He turned to inspect the inside of my locker door and smiled at his reflection in the small mirror. He ran his fingers over the stickers layered like a frame around it. His eyes moved down, to the photo.

"Anna's dad took it. He gave me a copy." I stepped forward, rolling up my sweatshirts. I quickly stuffed them in the bottom of my locker and moved to close the door, but Julian's hand pushed it back open.

"This was from the Winter League Championship?" Julian asked. "You're wearing your special sneakers."

I nodded.

"The trophy is so shiny."

I stood beside Julian and looked at the photo with fresh eyes. Frizzy hair framed my forehead, and my uniform stuck to my skin with sweat. My arm curled around Anna's neck, her arm wrapped around my shoulders. Anna had changed the elastics around her braces to our team colors (white and blue) just before the championship game. You could see them in the photo—all of them. Her smile was that big. My lips were parted in a smile, but . . .

"Your eyes," Julian whispered.

"What about them?"

"They're sad." He leaned in closer and then looked over at me.

I shook my head.

"No, Julian. They look worried because I *was* worried."

I pressed my sweatshirts down and stacked my socks on top.

"If you think opening my locker was tricky, closing it is even harder. Watch."

I reached for the papers and placed them on top of my mound of clothing. With my hairbrush holding everything in place, I whipped my locker closed, pulling my hand out at the last moment.

"It would be easier if it wasn't so full of clothing," Julian observed.

"I know."

Julian looked at me for a moment. I knew he was still thinking about the photo.

"Where do you want to go next?" I asked.

"Let's just wander," Julian suggested.

The hallway smelled of mop water, sneakers, and pencil clippings. Las Brisas hadn't changed a thing. Julian walked a little ahead of me, peeking into each classroom that we passed.

"Whoa, whose room is this?"

"That's Ms. Foley's room."

"Writing?" Julian asked as he pushed the door open and walked in.

"And reading."

Julian spun a book rack in a full circle. His fingers tapped the spines of the books in the classroom library. He then flopped on one of her beanbag chairs.

"Where do you sit?"

"We don't have assigned spots, but I try to sit by the windows."

Julian stood and gazed out into the courtyard. We were on the second floor, staring into the middle of a full sugar maple. It was bright green with spring now, but turned vibrant red in the fall.

"Do you have assigned spots at your school?" I asked.

"I kind of have to. The teachers have special gear for me—a lot of gear. It would be hard for them to move my spot from day to day. But I do move to different rooms depending on what I'm working on, kind of like you."

Julian walked over to Ms. Foley's desk and looked at her photos.

"Let's get going. I want to see more before time runs out."

We didn't linger long in my math classroom.

"Math teachers don't do much to decorate," I explained as we passed through the rows and rows of student desks. At the end of the hallway, we descended the stairs, all the way down to the basement and into my art room. The tabletops had been wiped clean but streaks of clay, markers, and paint remained.

"This is a lot like my art room," Julian said.

"Really?"

He nodded as he walked around the perimeter.

"We have a clay area and a paint area, and lots of sinks, but they are lower, and accessible."

I reached for his hand.

"Come see what I'm working on."

I guided Julian to the shelves in the back corner where my clay pinch pots were waiting for their glaze. The pots were as small as my fingertips, topped with tiny lids. Each lid was decorated with a tiny figure: a lion, a coiled snake, a bird's nest with eggs inside. Julian carefully plucked one from the back of the shelf. It was my cornucopia pot.

"They're so small."

"I know! Anna and I have been working on them together. We're trying to see how small we can get them, while keeping the lids recognizable."

Julian chuckled.

"What's so funny?"

"My pottery is the opposite. It's enormous. I'm working with my classmate, Dylan. We squeeze a ball of clay as hard as we can and make an imprint. Then we arrange them together. Right now, our sculpture kind of looks like a termite mound."

"How tall is it?"

"Let's see . . ." Julian squatted down and reached his hand up over his head. "It's about this high. I haven't worked on it since my big seizure, but pretty soon we'll have to build it out because we won't be able to reach higher from our chairs."

"I'd like to see it when it's complete," I said.

"I'd like you to see it, too."

We climbed up the steps to the main hallway, past the principal's office and nurse's office, toward the gym. Julian paused in front of the trophy case. A gigantic golden trophy sat front and center.

"Blue Eagles Girls' Basketball: Division One Champions," Julian read aloud. "This is your team's Winter League trophy, right?"

I nodded.

"This was the game you scored forty-three points and had thirty-two assists?"

I nodded.

Behind the trophy was a team photo. Coach had insisted

that I hold my MVP trophy for the photo. The team had insisted that I sit in the front. My smile had matched theirs.

"Your eyes are worried here, too." Julian placed his hand on my shoulder. "She meant to call and let you know," he said.

"Papa could have," I said, as I shrugged his hand off.

"But he doesn't think of things like that."

"That's not an excuse."

Julian stepped closer to the trophy case and looked at the collage of championship photos.

"I wanted to ask you about the game, but you know I—I can't." Julian's voice was soft. "And you never talked about it. Papa read me the article from the paper . . ."

I glanced at the photos and pointed to the glass.

"That one, with me stretched out across the floor, passing the ball to Alissa—I was pushed down by the forward on the other team. She wasn't called for a foul, but I didn't mind, because after Alissa caught the ball, she ran it in for a layup."

My finger moved to a photo of me shooting a three-pointer over my defender's outstretched arms. "This photo was just as the third quarter started. We were tied at halftime. Coach told us that we needed to come back strong."

"Looks like you did."

I nodded.

"You got an ice-cream cone when you joined us at the hospital," Julian offered. "I remember Papa got your favorite flavor—black raspberry."

I smiled.

"There's that smile again, like the one in these photos—with your mouth but not with your eyes." He stepped closer. "But now your eyes are sad, not worried."

"When I didn't see you at the game, Julian, when I couldn't find you or Mama or Papa in the crowd, I found Anna's dad at halftime and asked him to call home. He couldn't get hold of Mama or Papa. I watched him from the court. He kept calling through the entire second half.

"Maybe that's why I played so hard, to try to block the worry. After the game ended, after the trophies were awarded, everyone went home—except for Anna and her dad. He still couldn't get hold of Mama and Papa, so he took us for ice cream." I looked over at Julian. "I thought something bad had happened to you, something very, very bad. Finally, after my second Mudslide sundae, Papa called back. He said it was just your fever, and that it had gotten really high, really fast."

I turned my back to the photos and wiped my eyes on my sleeve.

"They forgot about me during my biggest game of the year. And I'm not supposed to complain about it, because what would that make me? Selfish."

"You're not selfish, Belle."

"I am, Julian. When I spoke to Papa on the phone and heard that you were okay, I didn't care how high your fever had gotten, or what tubes you'd had stuck inside you. I was angry. When I got to the hospital and Mama told me about your temperature— how you went from 103.4 degrees to 104.1 degrees during the ambulance ride—I interrupted her and told her about my free throws. When she told me about your seven-second seizure in the ER and the five-second seizure you had right before Anna's dad dropped me off, I pulled up my sleeves and my pant legs so I could show her the floor burn on my knees and elbows. And do you know what Mama said?"

Julian shook his head.

"She told me that I was being selfish."

"Belle, it's not selfish to want to be seen."

"And Papa? He was happy because I shared my ice-cream cone with him. He didn't know I had already had ice cream with Anna and her dad. He didn't think to ask what I'd been doing for the past hour, waiting to hear from them.

"It was like my game didn't even happen. No one asked how I'd played or how much I scored. They didn't even ask who won. I felt like I didn't matter." My voice trembled. The back of my throat burned. I wiped my eyes on my sleeve. "I know you were sick, Julian, and it was scary—but that game was a big deal for me, and no one noticed or cared."

"Belle—"

I put my hand up and Julian pressed his lips closed.

"I don't want to talk about the game anymore," I said as I started walking down the hallway, leaving the trophy case behind. "Come on, Julian. We're probably short on time. I'll take you to the cafeteria and show you where Anna likes to sit so she can stare at the boy she's too shy to talk to."

"What's his name again?" Julian asked, jogging a little to catch up.

"His name is Troy. She's had a crush on him since third grade."

"That's a long time," Julian said.

"I know."

"Belle—stop." Julian stepped in front of me. "Where do you keep your trophy? I've never seen it."

"It's in my closet."

"Can you show it to me sometime?"

I nodded and started walking again. The smell of ketchup and chicken fingers greeted us as I pushed the cafeteria doors open.

"Belle?"

"Yes, Julian?"

I turned around and looked at him, looked deep in his brown eyes, eyes that weren't sad or worried, but warm and filled with love. He hesitated.

"Are you going to ask another question about the Winter Championship? I told you I don't want to talk about it."

Julian's cheeks dimpled as he shook his head.

"You're making me nervous," I said, fighting a smile.

"What I'm wondering is . . . is there someone *you're* too shy to talk to?"

My cheeks grew warm and I inched closer.

"We might be in Las Brisas, having a heart-to-heart moment. But Julian, listen closely: I am not talking about crushes with you." I spun around and marched over to Anna's favorite seat.

"I'll take that as a *yes* then," Julian called out after me.

I stopped short on the sidewalk on my way out of school. Mama was standing next to our car and waving me over. My heart sped up as I walked closer. I let out a breath of relief when I saw that she was smiling and Julian was sitting in the backseat.

"Hey, Julian."

He lifted his head and looked at me. His lips quivered as he tried to smile.

"Julian has a checkup," Mama explained.

I opened the door and buckled myself in next to Julian.

"How was Julian's day?" I asked my mother.

Mama looked at me in the rearview mirror. Her eyes were wide with excitement.

"His teachers tracked only three seizures today."

"Wow, that's . . . that's so few."

"I know." She drummed her fingers on the steering wheel. "By this time yesterday, he'd had seven. So far today he's at four—including the one at breakfast. I've got a good feeling about the rest of the day. I think his new meds are really kicking in."

"Did he work on his clay sculpture today?" I asked.

"His what?"

"Julian is building a clay sculpture with Dylan."

Mama looked over at Julian, whose hands lay on his lap. His

head rolled toward the window.

"No, Isabelle. Julian is taking a break from art right now as we work on reducing his seizures." Her eyes caught mine for a few seconds. I knew better than to speak up.

Julian's body relaxed as Mama started the car. The engine always soothed him. Today, it seemed to knock him out.

"How was your day?" Mama asked as we left the school parking area.

"Good," I answered, watching Julian's breathing grow heavy.

"How'd you do on your math quiz?"

I thought about lying, but it just didn't feel right.

"I have it tomorrow," I said.

Thanks to her special gift, Mama's brain was able to hold countless bits and pieces of information. On top of all of Julian's seizure info, Mama remembered every one of my tests, assignments, and presentations. She had memorized the ridiculous llama dance I had performed when I was three. She could recite the birthday song I created for Papa's fortieth birthday—all seventeen verses of it. I only needed to mention a quiz once, and she'd remember the date and ask me how it went.

But that had changed since Julian's big seizure. Now, her memory was off.

"Everything all right?" I asked.

"Yes, Isabelle. I've just got a lot on my mind." She tightened her grip on the steering wheel. I pretended not to notice.

The drive wasn't long, but it took us out of town, across the falls, to a city nearby. Julian used to see doctors in regular doctor offices, but as he got older and his seizures continued, he met with special doctors in their special offices. These offices weren't in a clinic, or a cozy building. They were housed at the regional hospital, in the children's wing.

When I was little, I'd found the hospital exciting, with its shiny, waxed floors, the bright lights, and the elevators. I liked the warm receptionists, the eager nurses, and the never-empty baskets of stickers. The hospital became less magical as Julian's seizures continued and the potential mystery cure grew more distant.

For this visit, like every one before, Mama, Julian, and I wound our way through the hallways, up to the fourth floor, and through the automatic doors decorated with paper flowers.

I stood next to the gigantic fish tank. Two clownfish raced around a bubbling treasure chest; one bloated purple fish floated on the surface.

"We'll see you in a little bit, Isabelle," Mama said, kissing me on the forehead.

"Bye, Julian," I said, giving his hand a squeeze.

He always squeezed back, every doctor visit, for as long as I could remember. With his hand in mine, I waited. I laced my fingers in between his and moved in closer.

"Julian?"

"Isabelle." Mama's voice came as a sharp whisper. "None of this nonsense now."

My arm pulled back. I watched my mother wheel Julian toward the reception desk.

"Mama."

She paused and turned. "What is it, Isabelle?"

I stepped over quickly.

"Can I . . . can I see what the doctor does with Julian?"

She took a deep breath and brushed her curls behind her ears.

"It's just a lot of doctor talk. I don't think you'll find it that interesting," Mama said. "You should go back and get started on your homework."

"I'd rather go with you and Julian," I said.

"No, Isabelle." Mama's voice was firm. "With all the changes Julian's been through, I don't want any distractions during the visit."

"I help out at home; maybe I'll learn something useful. And I don't have any homework. Mrs. Harris wants us to finish up our science fair projects. I can't do that here."

Mama hesitated, and I could tell that I had a chance. "I'll be quiet, I promise."

"All right, then." She shrugged. "Come on."

A nurse led us to a small room. Mama wheeled Julian in and sat on a plastic chair. She let me sit on the examination table. The nurse pulled the curtain back and stepped into the hallway. A moment later, another nurse came in.

"Hey there, sleepyhead," she said to Julian as she checked his blood pressure and his temperature. She typed something into the computer, pulled a curtain around the door, and slipped out.

"Now what?" I asked.

"Now we wait for Dr. Holland," Mama said as she pulled a magazine off the shelf. A small mobile dangled above my head. I watched it spin, first clockwise, then counter. The heating vent turned on and blew warm air into the room—too warm for mid-May. The tissue paper on the table crinkled every time I moved. I held my breath, and tried to sit perfectly still.

That's when I heard the door latch open. The curtain pulled back. The doctor was tall with a few strands of hair brushed limply across the top of his head. His eyes were like water, but when he smiled at Mama and me, his eyes smiled, too.

"Good afternoon, Mrs. Perez. And this must be Isabelle." Dr. Holland shook my hand. He turned to look at Julian, who slouched in his seat, eyes closed. He turned back to my mother. "So please tell me, how's Julian doing?"

"Well," Mama said, taking a deep breath and rubbing her hands together as her left foot tapped the floor tiles, "he's been very tired, as you can see. But, in terms of his seizure activity, the past few days have been really good."

Mama pulled Julian's seizure journal out of her bag and handed it to Dr. Holland.

"He had thirty-six seizures on Sunday, the day he returned home. As you know, he averaged 21.2 seizures a day before his big seizure. On Monday, Julian had fourteen seizures. He had eleven on Tuesday. Tuesday morning, he only had seven—it was dinnertime when the rest came, just about five or ten minutes apart."

"That can happen." Dr. Holland nodded.

"Today Julian's only had four. As I was telling Isabelle, he had six at this time yesterday. No, wait"—she shook her head—"seven at this time yesterday."

Dr. Holland checked the journal and looked back at my mother.

"You've got quite a memory," he said.

"It's her special gift," I said.

Dr. Holland's thick eyebrows scrunched together as my mother's eyes narrowed.

"Special gift?"

I looked to my mother who gave a nod of consent, not agreement.

"She's got a magic memory. Papa's gift is that he can eat anything."

"And yours?"

"She's still searching for hers," Mama interrupted. "About the seizures . . ."

"Yes, yes. Let me check a few things first."

Dr. Holland closed the notebook and then moved closer to Julian. He took out a mini flashlight, pulled each of Julian's big beautiful eyes open, and shined the light inside. I wondered if Julian was seeing blurry blotches the way I do after someone shines a light in my eyes, but Julian didn't flinch or stir from his nap. The doctor held on to Julian's hands and moved his fingers around. He pressed a stethoscope to Julian's chest and his back. He took out Julian's chart and ruffled through the pages.

"Well, Mrs. Perez, I think you're starting to see the benefits of this new medication."

"Really?" Mama's voice sounded different. There was a touch of hope, too fragile and raw to grasp, but enough to sense.

"Yes." Dr. Holland flipped to a chart and showed it to my mother. "If the patient is taking to the new medication, there is a noticeable drop just about ten days in. You'll need to track the next few days so we can be sure."

"Absolutely." Mama nodded and chewed her lip. "So, this means . . ."

"We increase the dosage, little by little, starting next week. In many cases, patients taking this medication have five seizures or less each day. For some, they go away completely."

"Julian." Mama pulled his hand to her lips, peeled his fingers out of his fist, and kissed his palm. "Julian, did you hear that?"

Julian's chest rose up slowly and then fell as he let out a deep breath. A small drop of drool gathered at the corner of his mouth.

"Julian, sweetheart," she continued.

"Mama—" I began.

"Did you hear what the doctor said?" Mama whispered to Julian. She brushed his hair away from his face. She turned back to Dr. Holland. "He's just tired."

Dr. Holland nodded. "The most common side effect. Fatigue will be more pronounced with a higher dosage. I'll send the updated prescription to the pharmacy. Finish what you have and start the new dose next week. You can schedule a follow-up appointment at the desk."

"Mama?" My voice came out soft as a nudge, but she couldn't hear it. She released Julian's hand and reached for Dr. Holland's.

"Thank you, Dr. Holland. This is what we've been hoping for."

10

The tips of my fingers were black, but I could still see the curves and swirls of my fingerprints—spiraling like a snail's shell, a cinnamon bun, water racing down the drain.

"Heads up!" Julian called out as he passed the basketball. I caught it with both hands and dribbled in for a layup.

Julian quickly rebounded and dribbled out to half-court, the ball threading in and out of his legs.

"Wanna try a one-on-one match? I'll go easy on you, I promise."

"Don't," I said, trying to sound fierce.

Julian nodded, his dimples growing with his smile. Looking past me, he dribbled in hard for a layup. My sneakers squeaked against the gym floor as I tried to keep up. Julian drove past me and performed his signature move. His left hand spun the ball completely around his waist while his body soared toward the basket. His arm reached up in slow motion. The ball gently climbed to the rim and fell in.

"Okay, maybe you can go a *little* easy on me," I said, watching the ball swish through the net.

"How about this: Your baskets count for two points, mine for one?"

I considered his offer for a moment.

"Deal," I said. I held out my hand. In Las Brisas, Julian's handshake was firm and strong.

"First to ten?" I proposed, dribbling up to the half-court line.

He nodded. Julian's eyes were on mine, not on the ball.

I lunged forward. Julian kept up. I attacked the basket, turned to the side, and faded back for a jump shot. The ball bounced against the rim, up to the backboard, and then tumbled down. We both dove for the rebound, but I caught it first. Julian bent his knees, anticipating my next move. With the ball dribbling almost on its own, I faked left and then moved right for a layup.

Two points.

At the half-court line, Julian's eyes intensified. I reached in for the ball as he dribbled forward. Julian bounced the ball behind his back and raced past me for the basket. I felt a breeze trailing behind him. Standing at the top of the key, all I could do was shake my head.

"How'd you get so good?" I asked.

"From you," Julian said as he passed me the ball.

"Really?"

"You can't hear Mama and Papa from the bench, but during your games, they sound just like the announcers you hear on TV, telling me the play-by-play."

He cleared his throat and deepened his voice, adding a thick Mexican accent:

"Isabelle passes the ball to number four, who dribbles once and passes it back. Isabelle fakes a shot and runs in for a layup . . ."

His voice sounded just like Papa's.

And then he raised it and changed the accent a little:
"Arms up! Arms up! Stuff her, Isabelle, stuff her!"

This was a terrible impression of my mother, but the words were true. Mama was very competitive, and she loved it when I blocked the ball.

Julian continued. "I listen to what they say, how you move on the court. But, you're my real teacher. You tell me about every practice, and you tell me your game strategy at dinner. You tell me about the plays you had, the shots you made or missed—"

Julian abruptly stopped talking. He must have seen the puzzled look on my face.

"What?"

"Nothing." I wiped sweat from my forehead. "I didn't know you listened to me so closely."

"Well, not all the time." Julian smiled. "But I like basketball. I like going to your games. I like the smell of the court. I like the sound of the ball and the vibrations it makes when it hits the floor. The cheers from the crowd give me goose bumps, and I look forward to hearing your voice after the games. You're so excited, even after your losses."

We continued our one-on-one match and followed it with free throws.

My first shot fell through the net. Julian gave me a high five, but as our palms slapped together, I held on to his hand. Julian smiled and I saw the depth of his dimples.

Standing with Julian, framed by the blackness of Las Brisas, I remembered how he had sat in his chair just hours ago, shortly after his evening dose of medication. Mama had hugged me tight and kissed Julian's cheeks seven times, one for each seizure that had interrupted his day. Julian might have felt the kisses, but I wasn't sure. His breathing had turned deep. His eyes had been tightly closed. I had reached over and held his hand, which felt heavy inside mine.

In Las Brisas, Julian pulled his hand from mine and dribbled to the free-throw line. He lifted the ball up in his hands. He felt the weight of it in his palm before his first shot, his eyes clear and focused. His arms angled for a perfect shot. His body tensed as he prepared to release the ball. And just then, as sudden as a raw wind sneaking in before a storm, my eyes filled with tears. Even though I hadn't made a peep, Julian moved the ball down and turned around.

"Belle, what's wrong?" he asked.

I was crying. Heavy and hard. Snot oozed from my nose. I choked on my breath and my chest heaved.

Julian let the ball go. It bounced against the gym floor and rolled out of sight. Reaching out for my hand, he led me to the bleachers. He sat down beside me and wrapped his arm around my shoulders. He said nothing. He waited until I was ready, until I was done crying and had made sense of the tears.

He listened as I turned the tears into words.

"I love being here with you Julian. But . . ."

"What, Belle?"

"I miss spending time with you at home. You haven't been the same since you came back from the hospital. You're always asleep. Even when you're awake, you're not really awake.

"And what makes it so hard is that Mama's so happy—she's

more focused than ever. Your seizures are down to a handful a day. And that's what we've always wanted, right? We wanted you to live your life without being interrupted by your seizures. But now that they're almost gone, you're so sleepy. And Dr. Holland is increasing your dose next week. Do you know what that means? You'll just get sleepier. What happens then?"

"I didn't know about that." Julian frowned.

"That's because you were asleep for the whole visit with the doctor," I said, shaking my head. "I miss watching you play with your instruments. You can't build crafts or paint or use your therapy tools."

Julian slid his arm off my shoulder and knotted his hands together on his lap. He took a deep breath.

"I miss those things, too."

"I hate the seizures. I hate them." I turned to Julian. His brown eyes, the color so rich and warm and deep, looked inside of me.

"I know, Belle. Me, too."

"But Julian, I don't understand. Some people have seizures and they can still do everyday things. Why do yours have to be so bad?"

"No one knows, Belle. Mama, Papa, and all the doctors I've ever seen. No one knows. It's just the way it is."

I sniffled and wiped my eyes.

"It's just not fair, Julian . . ."

My words fell to the floor. I stared at the laces on my sneakers, sneakers from Las Brisas that fit my long slender feet perfectly.

"Belle?"

"Yes?"

"Life's not fair."

That just made me angry. I stood up and paced around the court.

"I want to play basketball with you at home, in our driveway." My voice was too loud.

"We do—"

"It's not the same, Julian." I practically spat these words out.

"Belle, I hear the ball as it slams against the backboard. I watch the rim shake when the ball misses the basket. I study you as you take each shot, the way your body becomes so still for a fraction of a second, preparing the ball, aiming, taking a breath.

"Just because I can't ride the rides at the county fair doesn't mean I don't like being there, watching the lights, hearing you laugh, smelling the crazy food Papa orders."

Julian stopped because I was shaking my head. It wasn't that I disagreed with what he said; it was just that those weren't the words I wanted to hear.

"I just feel bad, Julian. Why wasn't I born like you, or why couldn't we share it? Some days you could be like me, and some days I could be like you."

"Belle, it just is what it is."

I sat silently next to Julian.

He put his arm around my shoulders again and leaned his head against mine.

"Belle, at dinner you were telling Mama a story, but I couldn't follow what it was about. I listened to your voice and my eyes were getting so heavy. I hoped that if I listened hard enough, I would stay awake. And then I hoped that even if I fell asleep, I would remember what you were saying."

"What *was* I saying?"

"I don't remember." Julian looked down at his shoes. "I've been having so much fun with you in Las Brisas, but now that I think of it, the rest of this week has been a blur."

"Do you remember your music class?"

"Yes, Mrs. Pemberly isn't easy to forget. But what about the tambourine? Have we practiced?"

"I've tried. But your hands can't hold it," I explained.

"Because I'm asleep."

I nodded.

Julian pulled his arm away and put his head between his knees. I wrapped my arm across his back and squeezed him.

"What's going to happen to Las Brisas?" he finally asked.

"What do you mean?"

Julian lifted his head and looked at me.

"I—and now, we—visit places I've been to or heard about, remember? At some point, I won't be hearing about anywhere new. I—I don't mind visiting places I've been to before, but in Las Brisas I can see places I'll never get to, or experience them in different ways."

"The cenote . . ."

Julian turned his head away from me. "I may be losing my seizures, but it feels like I'm losing everything else, too."

The game clock on the wall suddenly switched on—a neon flash—and started counting down. Five minutes, twenty-three seconds. Five minutes, twenty-two seconds. Julian stood and found the ball. He batted it between his fingers.

"Belle, our time is almost up. How about a few more baskets?"

I turned and looked around. Darkness was creeping over the bleachers.

"There's never enough time," I said.

"No, there isn't. But there's always now."

I put my hands up just in time to catch the ball.

The following day, Mama's car pulled into the driveway earlier than usual. I tucked my basketball under my arm and stepped beneath the lilac bush. Even before the car was parked, the passenger door popped open and a pair of magenta heels poked out.

"Tía Lucy!" I exclaimed. The ball fell from my arm as I ran to the car.

"Isabelle, my darling, *Amorcita*." Tía scooted out of the car, adjusted the hem of her neon-yellow skirt, and kissed my cheeks. "My, how much you've grown. So tall and so beautiful—so much like me."

"Mama said you were coming *next* week."

"She decided to surprise us," Mama explained as she stepped out of the car.

"I had tickets for next week, but then I thought, why wait? Please, Isabelle, come and help me with Big Betty and Sanchita. They need to stretch their legs."

While Mama lifted Julian from the car and eased him into his wheelchair, I scooped the Chihuahuas out of their carriers.

"Don't worry about the rest of my things. Hernando can get them." Tía Lucy waved her hand dismissively as she carefully lifted a large white box from the car.

"How long are you staying?" I asked, holding the dogs close

to my chest. Their shivers rattled my ribs while their small black noses sniffed the spring air.

"I'm not yet sure. Santi is opening a new restaurant and he practically sleeps there. He'll probably do that until things are running smoothly. Once he's all set up, he'll give me a call and I'll fly back for the grand opening." Tía Lucy paused at the front door. "Hush, Isabelle. Let's surprise your father."

Tía Lucy slipped out of her high heels and tiptoed into the house. Four inches shorter, we were now the same height. Tía smiled and raised an eyebrow before peeking into the kitchen.

"Aye! Hernando, what are you eating?"

Papa leapt to his feet and stood in front of the table, his eyes searching for my mother.

"Inez, you said the Taco Queen wouldn't arrive for another week! I traded some shifts so that—"

"So that what?" Mama asked drily, wheeling Julian into the kitchen.

"So that . . ." I couldn't tell if Papa was searching for the right words or the wrong words.

Tía Lucy's eyes narrowed as she carefully placed the box on the kitchen table.

"It just means we'll have even more time together, Hernando." Tía Lucy smiled as she peeked at the plate hidden behind his back. "Chanchito, this is disgusting."

She grabbed the plate, which was filled with waffles, hot dogs, and French fries covered in swirls of mustard and maple syrup. Mama stepped away from Julian to inspect Papa's plate.

"Yes, that is disgusting. Hand it over."

Tía Lucy's eyes sparkled. Papa frowned.

"Now that your hands are free, you can go get my things. And the groceries. Papá is coming for his birthday dinner, no?"

Papa nodded as he trudged out the door, pausing only to kiss Julian on the top of his head and me on the cheek.

"Isabelle," Tía Lucy began, scooping Big Betty from my arms, "your mother told me all about your science fair project. I can't wait to see it."

"Julian has helped a lot."

"I'm sure he has." Tía Lucy batted her long eyelashes as she watched Mama wheel Julian to the kitchen.

"He inspired me," I said.

"I know," she said.

"Lucia!" Papa interrupted. "Why do you need to pack so much?" He pulled two enormous suitcases into the living room, sweat dripping down his brow.

"I just do." Tía Lucy winked.

"Nando!" Mama called out.

I knew her voice. Julian was seizing. Papa put the suitcases down and hurried into the kitchen.

"Isabelle?" Tía Lucy said, putting her hand on my shoulder.

"Yes?"

"How is Julian doing?"

"Didn't Mama tell you?" I peeked into the kitchen.

"She did. She told me what she sees. But I want to know what you see."

I watched Papa soothe Julian. Once he was finished seizing, Mama gave Julian a kiss and pulled out the notebook.

"How many today?" Papa asked.

"Five," she said.

Tía Lucy wasn't watching them. Her eyes were on me.

"He's not the same at all. He's asleep all the time," I said. "I miss him."

I started scratching Big Betty's ears in her favorite counter-clockwise manner. Mama knelt beside Julian as Papa stood and walked back out to the car.

"Julian's seizures interrupt his day," Tía Lucy said.

"Yes, but now his days are interrupted by his sleeping," I said. "Before, Julian had anywhere between fifteen and thirty seizures a day, but in between, he was awake and alert. I want his seizures to go away. I really do. But I don't like this."

"Have you told your mother how you feel?" Tía Lucy asked.

"Look at her, Tía. She's so relieved."

Mama stood at the counter staring at the seizure notebook. A few months ago, the pages were filled with so much ink that they curled in from the edges.

"Isabelle," Tía Lucy leaned in and whispered into my ear. "Do you know why I came early?"

"Because of Uncle Santi's restaurant. That's what you said."

"Oh, that's part of it. Trust me, he's a nervous wreck when a new restaurant opens. I should know; this is his seventeenth. But that's not the real reason why."

I stopped scratching Big Betty's ears and turned to Tía Lucy.

"I bought tickets to come when I heard about Julian's big seizure, because I wanted to help out my dearest sister. I wanted to check in on my sweet nephew. I wanted to be here for my father's birthday. But most of all, I needed to be sure my darling niece was getting the attention she deserves."

Papa stumbled into the house, four shopping bags in his arms, and a stalk of celery in his mouth.

"I thought you were outside too long. What have you eaten?" Tía Lucy scowled.

"Not too much," Papa mumbled as he chewed.

"Place those bags in the kitchen, Chanchito. I'm making Santi's famous Fajitas in a Flash for dinner tonight. I hope you haven't eaten any of the ingredients." Tía Lucy marched over to Julian and placed Big Betty on his lap. She draped his arms around the little dog's round belly. "My darling Isabelle, I want to hear more about your science fair project, but right now, your mom needs help in the kitchen."

"I'm off to work," Papa declared, flakes of Parmesan cheese drifting from his mustache. He leaned in and gave me a one-handed hug. "Save me some of that birthday cake."

"Good night, Papa." I hugged him back, ignoring the mango he was hiding from Tía Lucy.

"You should clean up your room, Isabelle. At least put all your dirty laundry in the hamper." My mound of laundry was more like a mountain range. "And don't forget to set up your things for tonight. You know how your tía keeps you up late talking. You might be too tired later on."

Panic seized my chest as I watched Papa leave the house. I had forgotten about that part of Tía Lucy's visits. I never minded sleeping in a sleeping bag in the corner of my room, but that was before Las Brisas. My heart raced.

"Inez, slice the onions so they are as thick as your finger," Tía Lucy advised. My eyes burned as I walked into the kitchen.

"Can I sleep in Julian's room tonight?" I asked my mother.

"Isabelle," Mama said. She took a deep breath and blinked quickly. The strong scent of onions filled the kitchen. "Where is this question coming from? You know I don't like his room getting cluttered. Now, go set up your things as usual."

"Thinner, Inez." Tía Lucy peeked over Mama's shoulder.

"You said as thick as my finger," Mama protested

"I must have meant *my* finger," Tía Lucy said with a shrug.

Upstairs I dragged the hamper out of the bathroom and left it in the hallway outside my room. I balled up my laundry. From across the room I made a dozen T-shirt jump shots, sprinted down the hallway for a few behind-the-back slam dunks (sweatpants), and finished with left-handed three-pointers (socks).

Once my room was clean, I pulled my sleeping bag out of my closet and found my pajamas in my dresser drawer. I unrolled my sleeping bag. Every time I shifted my weight, it felt like the floor was a violin playing out of tune. There was no way I was going to sneak past Sanchita and Big Betty. They'd bark and alert Tía Lucy.

I chewed my fingernail and searched for a solution as my mother's voice and the smell of spices drifted up the stairs.

"I'm putting Julian in his room to rest."

That's when I knew Abuelito had pulled into the driveway.

Abuelito always leaned into the door, pulling at the knob, sending shivers down my spine. I imagined the old wooden door pushing back with all of its weight. It scraped the floor and screeched, like the time Papa backed over our recycling bins and they lodged under the car. Papa drove me all the way to preschool before he realized what had happened, and it took him the entirety of my school day to pull them back out.

From my bedroom, I felt the thumps of Abuelito's clomping shoes and the utter silence that followed each step. That is, until the Chihuahuas found him.

"Surprise!" Tía Lucy called out.

Peeking around the bend in the steps, I watched Tía Lucy kiss Abuelito on his stubbly cheeks. She buzzed around him like a famished mosquito, helping with his coat, his cap, and his shoes. Tía Lucy helped slide his feet into a pair of slippers. Mama brought him the small cup of coffee he always asked for but never finished.

I made my way down, sat on the last step, and waited. Abuelito sat at the table with his hands resting on the top of his cane, sipping coffee, adding more sugar with each sip. Mama rambled on about this and that, talking about Papa and my grades. The routine of the visit was the same as every other Abuelito visit.

I craned my neck and looked into Julian's room, where Julian sat. Mama always parked his chair in just the right spot. She could view him from the stove while she stirred a pot of *frijoles*, or from the table where she made small talk with Abuelito.

I pulled my knees up to my chin. I looked at the clock and the too-many hours until bedtime, puzzling over how I'd devise my escape route to Las Brisas.

"Isabelle, stand up," Mama's voice commanded. "Your

grandfather's here. Come over and wish him a happy birthday."

"Happy birthday," I said.

I didn't walk to the table first. I stopped and stood at the threshold of Julian's room. Julian was less droopy than before. His evening dose was just over an hour away. His afternoon medications were wearing off, and his energy was returning. His right hand slowly pushed dried beans around his tray, carving shapes and writing abstract letters with his fingers.

"Isabelle," Mama called again. "Come sit down."

I took one last peek at Julian and sat down at the table beside Abuelito.

"Inez, it's time," Tía Lucy instructed, nodding at the skillet. Mama took it from the stovetop and placed it on an oven mitt on the table. Uncle Santi's fajitas looked more glorious than a Thanksgiving turkey.

"Where's the boy?" Abuelito asked my mother.

"Julian? He's in his room," Tía Lucy said.

He's always in his room when you come over, I thought.

"What brings you here? It's not June," Abuelito asked Tía Lucy.

"I thought I'd surprise Inez and the kids with a little visit. And I couldn't miss my father's birthday!"

"Surprise? That seems silly to me," he grumbled.

Tía Lucy tsk-tsked.

Mama continued to hurry about the kitchen. She set the places at the table and scooped the frijoles. Tía Lucy served up our plates while Mama wheeled Julian over.

"Hey, Julian," I said. His eyes searched for me. I waved and he gave a groggy smile.

Abuelito wasted no time digging into his meal while Sanchita shivered in Papa's seat. Tía Lucy snuck bites of chicken and tortilla to Big Betty. She caught me watching.

"Now you know why Betty's so big. It's because I can't say no when she gives me her look. Isn't that right, Big Betty? Show me the look."

Big Betty turned her head all the way to the side, so her pointy ears tickled her chubby Chihuahua shoulders. Then she turned her head again to the other side.

Mama's plate remained empty as she swiveled her seat around and connected Julian's feeding tube.

"Time to eat, Julian," she whispered.

Abuelito took a big bite, rocked himself out of his seat, and meandered to the kitchen window. He chewed, gazing out at the wind socks and pinwheels. Once Julian's machine began pumping, Abuelito's back straightened and he returned to his food.

"You didn't make these tortillas. They taste like someone made them with their feet," he grumbled.

Mama rolled her eyes.

"Aye, Papá! I didn't have time," Tía Lucy said. "But I'll make some this week and bring them over."

"They're from the supermarket," Mama explained.

"They taste like cardboard."

"Your grandmother made the best tortillas," Tía Lucy explained. "She saved the best ones for Papá."

Abuelito nodded and continued eating.

Mama served herself and scooped more frijoles onto

Abuelito's plate. I watched the gray and silver stubbles ripple on his neck. I watched the way he balled up his paper napkin in his hand until it was brown and greasy and perfectly round. I watched the way Mama sat too straight, her eyes flicking between Abuelito, Tía Lucy, and Julian, and sometimes me.

Every now and then, Abuelito stole a glance at Julian; he'd make it casual, like he was checking the time on the clock or pretending as though he'd heard something coming from behind. His eyes lingered.

Tía Lucy didn't notice. She was focused on feeding Big Betty.

Mama didn't notice. She was too busy concentrating. During Abuelito's visits, Mama's special gift of foresight kicked into high gear. She could sense seizures well before they happened, as if she could feel the tremor approaching. Sure enough, before I realized anything was amiss, Mama leapt out of her seat and attended to Julian.

As Mama softly whispered to Julian, the wrinkles around Abuelito's face grew more pronounced, lines worn into sandstone. You could get lost in those wrinkles.

"That makes six today," she said, and marked it in Julian's notebook.

"Papá," Tía Lucy said, placing her hand on Abuelito's arm, "has Isabelle told you about her fabulous engineering project?"

I dropped my fork and looked up at Abuelito. The surprise on his face must have matched mine.

"I—I haven't told him. I just started it this week," I stammered.

Abuelito ate another bite, his interest fading. Tía Lucy sat up straighter.

"Your granddaughter has created a wind turbine that serves up popcorn." Tía Lucy winked at me. "It sounds amazing. She's presenting it tomorrow in the early afternoon. I'm sure she'd be honored if you could come."

"I can't. I have an appointment." He slurped some coffee.

"That's too bad." Tía Lucy took a delicate bite and turned to me. "Your grandfather could build anything he wanted when he was a young man."

"Lucia . . ." Abuelito grumbled.

"He was also incredibly athletic." Tía Lucy leaned in and whispered, "It's hard to see that in him now."

Mama returned to her seat and ate quickly as Tía Lucy cleared the table. Soon, they carried over a chocolate cake glowing with dozens of candles. Abuelito's eyes reflected the flames, but didn't brighten. It took him three tries, but he finally blew all the candles out.

"*Ochenta y dos* . . ." he muttered in Spanish as Mama started slicing.

Mama didn't meet his eyes. She handed out pieces of cake, and then returned to the counter to mix Julian's medications. Tía Lucy took a bite of the cake, a puzzled look on her face.

"Papá? Why are you still counting?" Tía Lucy shook her head. "Your grandson is right there!"

Abuelito didn't look to where Tía Lucy was pointing. Instead he took a bite of his cake.

Tía Lucy's words echoed in my mind and my nose twitched.

"What're you talking about?" I asked, turning to my mom and to Tía Lucy.

"Oh, it's just your abuelito, still in the dark ages." Tía Lucy took an enormous bite of cake and dabbed her mouth with a napkin. "He's waiting for a boy."

"A boy?"

"Lucia . . ." Mama warned.

Tía Lucy responded by leaning in close to me, though her voice was much louder than a whisper.

"Your abuelito always wanted a brother, to play ball with, but instead he was blessed with six sisters. Can you imagine his disappointment? Every birthday he wished for a brother. Isn't that right, Papá?"

Abuelito grunted and took another bite of cake.

"When he was married he wished for sons, but your *abuelita* gave birth to two daughters—your mother and me. No sons. So, every birthday he'd count the years and the waiting continued." Tía Lucy paused to take another bite. "He's still sore at Santi and me, because our babies aren't the human kind."

"But he has Julian." I pushed my cake away. "Mama?"

Mama's eyes met mine. She shook her head.

I peeked at Julian and turned back to watch Abuelito take another bite of cake. Tía Lucy watched me closely, the flame now burning in her eyes.

I stood up and marched over to Julian.

"Julian." His head was resting on his shoulder. "Julian, please wake up."

I shook his shoulders gently. His eyelashes lifted.

"Can you hear me, Julian?" I asked. Once open, Julian's eyes searched for mine. When they found me, they opened wider.

And he smiled. "Let's play some catch."

Mama kept Julian's box of therapy toys in the back of his closet. I swung the door open, stooped down, and dug around until I found a tennis ball. I squeezed the ball tight as I walked into the kitchen.

Abuelito straightened and looked over at me.

Tía Lucy turned her chair to get a better view. Mama closed the caps on half a dozen medicine bottles and walked over to me.

"It's time for his medication, Isabelle," she said.

"No, Mama. Not yet."

"Isabelle." She stepped closer. "Julian's medication is—"

"I know, Mama. I know how important it is for him. I've known that my whole life. But I want you to wait. Just wait five minutes."

"Isabelle . . ."

"Inez." Tía Lucy draped Sanchita across her shoulders and placed Big Betty in my mother's seat. "Let Isabelle explain."

I smiled at Tía Lucy and cleared my throat.

"Julian's awake and I want to show you something. I want to show Abuelito something."

"No, Isabelle." Mama shook her head. Her eyes were deep with disappointment. "His medicine can't wait. You know that. And your grandfather is about to leave."

She brought over the syringe, lifted up the hem of Julian's pajama shirt, and connected the syringe to his feeding tube. At the table, I watched Abuelito shield his eyes. When Mama finished, she looked at me again, the disappointment still showing on her face.

I unlocked the wheels of Julian's chair, pushed him over to Abuelito, and removed his tray.

"Isabelle," Mama said fiercely.

"Just like last night," I whispered into Julian's ears. "But with a tennis ball, okay?"

I uncurled Julian's right hand, moved his thumb to the side, and placed the ball in his palm. Julian wrapped his fingers around the tennis ball.

Taking a few steps back, I held my hands open in front of me.

"Keep your eyes open, everyone," I announced.

Julian's fingers gently brushed the fuzz. He smiled and his cheeks dimpled. His left hand dropped to his lap as his right arm pulled back.

My heart pounded in my chest. I looked back at Abuelito, whose eyes were pinned on Julian. Mama's face was guarded, but I didn't have time to stop and wonder why. I turned my focus back to Julian. His eyes were different. The brown got warmer. He sat up straighter. This wasn't Julian from Las Brisas, this was just Julian, the Julian I've always loved.

And then he flicked the tennis ball.

His arm swung and he released the ball at just the right time. It flew from his fingers and hit me on my shoulder.

"Ouch!" I laughed as I bent down to pick it up. "Great pitch, Julian!"

The towel dropped from my mother's hand. The Chihuahuas barked but Tía Lucy didn't shush them. Abuelito's eyes shifted to me. They were haunting.

"Want to see another one?" I asked.

Julian's arm fell down on his lap with his fingers curled slightly open. I pressed the tennis ball into his hand and backed away until I was several feet away from him. Julian slowly moved his hand into pitching position.

"I'm going to catch this one, Julian—just watch me," I said.

Mama scooped up Big Betty and scratched her back a little too forcefully. There was a glitter in her eyes—or maybe tears. I couldn't tell because I couldn't take my eyes off of Julian's pitching hand. Abuelito whispered something, something too soft to hear.

Julian flung the ball at me. It arced through the air and I caught it.

Before the next pitch, Mama pulled up a chair beside Abuelito. She tucked her hand inside his. Tía Lucy pulled up a seat as well. Her dogs snuggled into her lap, while Julian and I played catch for our audience. They applauded every throw. I moved even farther away, and Julian adjusted his throw accordingly. By the last few throws, I had my back pressed against the front door.

And then I saw it. A shadow passed before Julian's eyes. The next pitch was off. I moved forward to catch it, but it slipped through my fingers and bounced around my toes. When I pressed the ball back into his hand, Julian's grip trembled. His fingers twitched. His lips moved and he tried to speak.

"It's okay, Julian." I leaned in and brushed his curls to the side. "It's okay. You'll be fine. Your medicine is kicking in. It's just your medicine."

The ball rolled from his hand and I let it tumble to the floor because his hand had found mine, and my fingers would not let go.

I pressed my forehead to his.

"It's okay, Julian. It's okay." I kissed his cheek. "See you soon."

"Isabelle."

I looked up.

Abuelito was cradling the tennis ball like a piece of fruit. He stood and brought the ball over to Julian. Abuelito tucked it into the space between Julian's leg and the chair. He stooped and kissed Julian on the forehead. He kissed me, too, his lips soft, his stubble scratchy.

Mama and Tía Lucy walked Abuelito to his car. I wheeled Julian to his room, took out his pajamas, and placed them on his bed. When Mama didn't return right away, I took a washcloth out of the linen closet and ran it under warm water in the bathroom sink.

"Those were great throws," I said as I gently wiped Julian's face and neck. I brushed his hair off to the side of his forehead. His breathing deepened and his head sank into his shoulders.

"I'm sorry, Julian," I whispered. "I'm sorry I didn't do something sooner. It just took me a while to realize—"

But Mama had returned, so I said no more.

Together we tugged Julian's clothes off and slipped his pajamas on. Mama angled Julian's bed.

"Mama?" I began.

"Yes, Isabelle?"

"Why do you hide Julian from Abuelito?" I asked.

"Isabelle . . ." Mama's voice faded.

"You keep Julian far away. You don't talk about him. You've been telling everyone else how many seizures he's down to, but tonight you didn't tell Abuelito."

"I guess I . . ." She pulled down the shades and dimmed the lights. ". . . I guess I get afraid."

"Afraid of what?"

"Of so many things." Her arms tightened. "I'm afraid that Julian's seizures will scare Abuelito away, or that they'll go on too long. It's hard not knowing what will happen next. I think I'm afraid of that, too."

"I'm not afraid," I whispered.

Mama looked down at me. Her eyes were warm and deep and filled with love.

"Sí, Isabelle. You're not afraid. Thank goodness for that." She kissed my forehead. "Fear is worse than Julian's seizures. Fear keeps all of his beauty and possibilities hidden."

"You know what also keeps his possibilities hidden, more than his seizures?"

"What?"

"Sleeping through the whole day."

Mama pulled back and her eyes hardened.

"I know you care for your brother, Isabelle, but it's your father, the doctors, and I who make his medical decisions."

Mama stood and switched Julian's monitor on. She paused beside Julian, who was already fast asleep.

"Things were very scary in the beginning, Isabelle, when Julian was first diagnosed. Bad brain scans, bouts of pneumonia that wouldn't go away, visits to the doctor that turned into weeklong stays in the hospital. Things are much better now, but remembering all that is part of what makes me afraid." She looked across the room at me. "Time for bed, Isabelle."

Upstairs, Tía Lucy brushed Sanchita's teeth while I pulled on my pajamas and slipped into my sleeping bag.

"Isabelle," Tía Lucy said, peering down at me, "your mother told me that Julian's teachers okayed his dismissal, so he can leave school early and help out at your science fair."

"Well, that's good," I said. "Julian's a big part of my project, and he really wants to come."

"I checked the boxes in the garage after Papá left, and it looks like you're ready to go."

"I am." I paused, toying with my next words. "Tía Lucy, why is Abuelito so grumpy? He never seems to enjoy himself."

She tucked Sanchita in beside me and began brushing Big Betty's teeth.

"Isabelle, your abuelito has been through a lot in his life," she said. Her voice was soft and smooth.

"So has Julian."

Tía Lucy nodded and cleared her throat.

"Did your mother ever tell you about Abuelito's amazing hands?"

I shook my head.

She leaned in close, took one of my hands in hers, and turned it over slowly. She traced the lines and creases, wiggled my fingers around.

"Your abuelito could do anything with his hands. They were *his* special gift. He could fix cars, refrigerators, clocks. He was also a great baseball player—a pitcher. He could've made it to the major leagues."

"Really?" I had a hard time picturing my ancient, slumped-over Mexican grandfather as a major league pitcher.

"Really. But he had an accident when he was eighteen," Tía Lucy continued. "He was fixing up a beat-up car for your abuelita, as a surprise for her high school graduation."

She let my hand slip out of hers. She paused and flexed her fingers before she rubbed them together.

"Your abuelito was working underneath the car when the jack gave out. A tire crushed his hand." I closed my eyes, imagining the impact. Tía Lucy continued, "Your abuelita held on to his bloody and broken hand as they rode in the ambulance. It was terribly damaged, but he squeezed her hand so tight. When the nurses wheeled Abuelito into the operating room, they practically had to break his fingers to separate their hands. Abuelito was so afraid."

"Julian's not afraid of hospitals," I said, smoothing out my sleeping bag.

"He's brave like you." Tía Lucy took a breath and continued her story. "When your abuelito woke up from surgery, his hand was lifeless. He could lift it, but the fingers barely moved. He said it was like his hand had been replaced with a lead glove. The loss was tremendous. Hours earlier his hands were magic. After the surgery, his future changed forever. It was many years before he could hold a pencil and write, but he never played baseball or fixed a car again."

"What went wrong?" I asked.

Tía Lucy shrugged.

"Abuelito was just a poor Mexican boy on the operating table," she said, a hard edge to her smooth voice. "I suspect the surgeon felt he'd done a good-enough job. He probably felt he had better places to be on a Sunday afternoon."

I thought of Abuelito, struggling to tie his shoes each week. A tight sourness spread in the pit of my belly.

"I think . . ." Tía Lucy paused and wiped her eyes. "I think your abuelito has always waited for someone who could pitch for him."

We sat in silence for what felt like forever. Except for Sanchita and Big Betty, that is. They were now tucked into the sleeping bag beside me. Their shivering had stopped, replaced with squeaky snores.

"He never talks about baseball," I finally said, looking up as Mama stepped into my room.

"That was many, many years ago," Mama said.

"Would he be happy if I played baseball instead of basketball?" I asked.

Mama considered this for a minute as she sat down beside Tía Lucy.

"He's never come to any of my basketball practices or games," I added.

"He's set in his ways, Isabelle," Tía Lucy said.

"The problem is, Abuelito doesn't think of all the things Julian *can* do; he only thinks of the things Julian can't do," I said.

"Yes, Isabelle." Mama nodded. "You believe in Julian. You always have. It's your special gift."

"No, Mama. It's not a special gift to believe in Julian. You don't have to believe in him to see what he can do." My voice was growing louder than it should have, but I couldn't help it. "Julian can throw a ball. He can hold pinwheels, make art with clay, and keep rhythm with his tambourine. He listens to my stories and he smiles when I tell him jokes."

My head ached with frustration. I shook my head to clear my thoughts. Abuelito waited and waited for a boy, and he finally got one. But the boy he got came with shivers and shakes, not pitches and strikes. And then he got me, yet another girl.

"None of us like that Julian has seizures, not even Julian," I said. "But if all we do is focus on them, then they win. We miss out on all the possibilities." My fists tightened. "I know you don't like me talking about medicine, but Mama"—I blinked hard and fast to keep my tears away—"Julian used to be able to do so many things, and now he can't anymore. And it's not because of his seizures—it's because he's sleeping all the time."

"Isabelle. I asked you—"

"I know, Mama. But think about it. You've counted seizures all week, but have you tracked how many times Julian has laughed, or played, or made music?"

"Isabelle, not tonight!" Mama stood up. "One more word from you and Julian will not attend your science fair. I've had enough! You are his little sister, a twelve-year-old girl, not a doctor." She closed the door firmly behind her as she left.

"Life's not always fair," Tía Lucy whispered.

"And it's always less fair for Julian."

"It's not a competition, Isabelle," Tía Lucy said. Her voice was guarded. "But your mother *is* missing some obvious details. Your special gift isn't believing in Julian, or even helping others believe in him. Your special gift is seeing possibilities." Tía Lucy smiled as she looked down at me. "I want to tell you another story."

"Okay." I wrapped my arm around Big Betty's warm belly as she stretched in her sleep.

"We once lived in a small, run-down house. It had three rooms, hot water—sometimes—and foggy windows. But your mother and I didn't mind, because it was smack-dab in the middle of an orange grove. There were rows of trees as far as we could see. They stretched out across the street and wrapped around the back of our house."

"Mama told me about this house."

"Did she tell you that we hid in the trees?"

I shook my head.

Tía Lucy's eyebrows arced high as she leaned back.

"Your mother and I were always in trouble. We'd run through our mother's clean laundry while it was hanging on the line, kicking up dust until the bottom edges were caked with dirt. We'd sneak fresh tortillas—your mother was the best at sneaking them. She'd take them from the bottom when our mother wasn't looking. Aye! Your abuelita would get so mad!"

"What would she do?"

"She'd pull out the hairbrush."

"Hairbrush?"

"Yes. Your abuelita had a round wooden hairbrush. She'd chase us around the house. She was fast, but we were good at slipping out of her hands, and we would run into the orange grove.

"*¡Sinvergüenza!* she'd come out yelling. We were shameless!"

Tía Lucy laughed so hard that Sanchita and Big Betty hopped out of the sleeping bag and started barking.

"Oh, my babies, did I wake you up?"

"Then what happened?" I asked.

"After she'd scolded us for having no shame, she would leave us in the trees and go back inside. But we knew the coast wasn't clear. Not yet. So we would run deep into the orange grove and climb up high in the leaves. Your mother and I laughed so hard I was afraid we'd fall out. We'd wait until it got dark and we could hear Papá's pickup coming. He would park it so we could see the headlights flickering through the leaves, lighting his way to us."

"Abuelito?"

"Yes. We'd tumble from the branches like ripe fruit and land in his arms. *You smell like flowers,* he'd tell your mother. *You smell like sunshine,* he'd tell me."

"He said things like that?"

"He did." Tía Lucy nodded. "Your mother and I would fight over which hand we'd hold on to during our walk back home. The skin in the middle of his broken hand was so soft and the pulse so strong." Tía Lucy opened my palm and studied its lines. "His scars healed once before. They can heal again."

We sat in quiet for a while.

"You've been studying the wind?" she finally asked.

"Yes. I've researched facts on wind, the wind gods from different cultures, and wind instruments. And then I constructed a wind turbine."

"That's impressive, Isabelle. You and Julian sure do a lot together, even though nothing as mischievous as what your mother and I used to do."

"That's not true."

"It isn't?"

I sat up straighter.

"Did Mama tell you about Julian's April Fool's joke?"

"No, she didn't."

I sat up on my knees and smiled at the memory.

"A little while ago I realized that when Julian hums, it sounds like the microwave. After school, for weeks, I had him practice his hum and then coached him to make a beeping noise. He has a hard time with words, but he makes so many different sounds. He had to get the right beep and time the pause between the beeps.

"On the first day of April, during breakfast, I wheeled Julian near the microwave. He hummed, then beeped, and Mama put down her coffee and opened the microwave door. We did it three more times until Julian started coughing—that's what happens when he laughs too much, and finally Mama figured it out. She had us trick Papa when he got home."

"That's a pretty good April Fool's." Tía Lucy smiled.

"I know! It was great. Papa tried to get him to make a flushing toilet sound. Julian tried and he couldn't quite get it right, but that didn't matter, because once Julian made the noise, he'd start laughing and his smile was so big and toothy that we laughed anyway."

"What sound is he working on now?"

"Besides snoring?"

"Isabelle." She shook her head slowly.

"The sound that grass makes in the wind, the sound of his pinwheels spinning, and the sound of the gusts on top of Mount Washington. He practiced all this while helping me with my science fair project. And then he had his big seizure."

Tía Lucy was quiet for a moment.

"You've got a big day tomorrow," she said, unzipping her suitcase. She pulled out a long lacy nightgown and looked at me from the corner of her eye. "How about . . . how about you take your sleeping bag and go downstairs? I'm sure Julian would love your company."

"What?" I blinked in surprise. "Won't Mama know?"

"I'll distract her in the morning so you can make it seem like you were up early, preparing for the science fair."

I jumped out of my sleeping bag and gave Tía Lucy a big hug. "Gracias."

"Sweet dreams, Isabelle."

12

"Hey there, Julian," I whispered, slipping his hand inside mine. I looked over at the pinwheel, nestled among the pencils in the cup. I sat down on the edge of his bed. My mother's footsteps shuffled overhead.

"Tía Lucy told me about the orange groves that she and Mama used to play in, when they were young." I squeezed his hand with my fingers. "Maybe Las Brisas can send us there. We can run through the rows of trees and climb them."

I squeezed his hand again, but he didn't squeeze back.

"Where else could we go?" I asked. Julian's breathing was deep and rhythmic. I sat on Mama's chair and closed my eyes. "What about that beach with all the tide pools—the one in the cove? We should go when the tide is pulling out and dig for clams."

I let go of Julian's hand and opened my eyes.

"Remember how I pushed your chair into the low tide and the wheels got stuck? The seaweed was wrapped between the spokes. Papa was so mad at me, but then you started laughing. He scooped you out of your chair and we sat in the wet sand while he freed your chair. You laughed the whole time."

I ran my hands over the stitching on his quilt.

"We wouldn't have to worry about seaweed and stuck chairs in Las Brisas." I picked up his hand again and continued. "How about up the steps of the Pyramid of the Sun? Walking down the—"

Just then, the scent of orange tickled my nose. I looked over at the pinwheel. I watched it spin.

"Belle?"

"Right here."

Julian's hand held on to mine as he sat up.

"You snuck past the dogs?"

"I didn't have to. Tía Lucy let me come down."

Julian pulled his covers back, slid down, and knelt beside me.

"Thanks for playing catch, Belle."

"Anytime." My eyes found his. "Where do you think we'll go tonight?"

"I never know," Julian whispered. "I don't mind the mystery." He looked at me, and his expression changed. "What's wrong?"

"Nothing." I couldn't shake off the frustration and sadness I'd heard in Mama's voice. But the smell of oranges helped me push it aside.

Just as I leaned into him, Julian straightened. His head turned to the wall and he squinted.

"What is it?" I asked.

"I don't know . . . something . . . something moved on the wall."

And then I saw it—a flash from the corner of my eye. A tiny gold butterfly peeled itself off the wall, leaving behind a shadowy imprint. As we watched its jumpy flight to the ceiling, more butterflies emerged from the walls, creating a soft breeze and a rhythmic drumming sound. They gathered in the middle of Julian's room, a cyclone of golden wings.

"Come on, Belle."

Julian pulled me to my feet and we slipped inside the spiral. Julian's room blurred as the butterflies flew faster, pulling us up into the air. My toes searched for the carpet. My breath caught in my chest, but released when Julian's eyes met mine.

We traveled into a sky of budding blue, over streetlights and headlights, the spring air running through my hair. When the butterflies finally let us down, my feet pressed into warm packed earth.

Julian and I were standing on a wide path lined with agave plants, their thick, spiky stalks reaching out like upturned jellyfish.

We walked. The air was fragrant, the sun's warmth, a promise.

"Belle—" Julian pointed up ahead, to the horizon, to the haze of the rising sun, to the shadow rising in the dust.

"La Pirámide del Sol!"

We ran down the path and found ourselves in the middle of the ancient ruined city of Teotihuacan, surrounded by small temples and stone structures, with the pyramid before us.

"How many steps?" Julian asked.

I looked up.

"Papa said two hundred and forty-eight."

Julian's cheeks dimpled.

"Then we'd better get started."

The steps were narrow and steep, the stones sharp under our feet. We knew that time in Las Brisas moved quickly, sometimes too quickly. We climbed up to the second landing before pausing. I stretched my legs, and Julian rolled the sleeves of his pajama top up to his elbows.

"When I was little, Papa talked about taking me here. He

said he'd carry me in a backpack so I could see the view." His eyes squinted in the morning light. "I guess, in the end, he was too scared to take me so far from home."

Dawn greeted the ruined city, as long, dark shadows striped the earth. The stillness of the ruins would have been unsettling had it not been for the breeze—coaxing and gentle.

"Mama's mad at me," I said, feeling relief as the words spilled from my mouth.

"What?" Julian turned to me, his eyebrows scrunched. "She never gets mad at you."

"Oh, she's mad now."

"Why?"

"I told her that I don't like your new medicine. I told her that seizures are interruptions, but sleeping all day is worse."

"Huh." Julian scratched his forehead. "When did you tell her this?"

"At bedtime, in your room."

"I don't remember." Julian's eyebrows pinched together and his voice softened. "I must have been sleeping."

Julian didn't look at me, his eyes reaching out far, to the edges of the city, and then back up the sides of the stone pyramid.

"You're having fewer seizures with this new medicine, but there's also very little to interrupt," I said. "Unless it's a dream, I guess."

"I'm not dreaming. Not really." Julian started up the next set of steps.

"What do you mean?" I followed quickly behind.

"It's hard to describe, Belle. You know how music can

interrupt your dream, or become part of it?"

"Yeah." I smiled. "Papa's good-morning songs are the worst. He thinks they're like Mrs. Pemberly's."

"I know! It doesn't matter what I'm dreaming of. Once that song enters my dream, it becomes embarrassing and awkward." Julian paused and looked at me. "That doesn't happen any-more—not with music, or with voices. When I'm out, I'm out."

I wanted to make a joke about Papa's voice, his poor pitch and terrible rhymes, but that wasn't what mattered. Julian was missing out on everything: our after-school time, our dinner conversations, Papa's silly moments.

Julian frowned and took the steps two at a time. My legs burned as we walked up to the next landing.

"Can I tell Mama that I've spoken to you, and you don't like sleeping all day?"

"No, you can't." Julian picked at his fingernails.

"She can't come to Las Brisas?" I ventured.

"No, she can't. You believe, Belle. I think that's why you can come. No one else believes in me the way you do." Julian turned to me. "I know my brain isn't perfect, but I miss what it used to be able to do. I feel so far removed from myself, Belle—who I used to be, who I worked so hard to be."

I kept my eyes down as I spoke in a careful, even tone.

"There's something I've been meaning to talk to you about."

"What is it, Belle?"

My stomach ached with a sour sadness that burned my throat. I crouched down and hugged my knees.

"What if I'm only able to come to Las Brisas with you *because* of what's happening at home?"

"What do you mean?"

"Julian," I said, rubbing my palms across the stone step, jagged and gritty, to ward off the tears burning in my eyes. "What if I'm only able to come here because we can't do things together at home anymore?"

Julian squatted beside me. He bit down on his full lips.

"What makes you think that?"

"It makes sense, doesn't it?"

"Yes." He nodded. "The pinwheel?"

"We were working on it when your big seizure struck. And we couldn't work on it when you came back, because you were always sleeping."

Julian's eyes pinched shut as he continued to nod.

"I have been wondering what changed—what happened to suddenly allow you to join me in Las Brisas."

"You've been in the hospital dozens of times. I've snuck down and checked on you before. But nothing ever led me to Las Brisas. Until now."

Julian's body sank.

"It's so much fun having you here with me." Julian ran his hand through his dark curls.

"We have fun at home together."

"We used to." He rubbed his temples and nodded.

Julian looked up to the top of the pyramid, down to the ruins below, and back at me. I slipped my hand in his and pulled him up.

We walked hand in hand, in silence, as we neared the top.

I felt like I was getting blisters on my feet. I brushed sweat from my forehead and hair out of my eyes, but I never let go of Julian's hand.

And then suddenly, the sky greeted us.

The top of the Pyramid of the Sun was a rounded square, crowned with chipped stones. The view of the Mexican valley was incredible. Mountains in the far distance, the ruins below. The wind rubbed our backs and kissed our cheeks.

When the butterflies returned, I knew it was time to go back home. They drifted from above, swirled around us, and the smell of citrus filled my nose.

I didn't return to my bedroom. I didn't stay and watch Julian sleep. After we returned from Las Brisas, I took his tub of tennis balls and snuck out to the garage.

In the light of a single bulb, I peeled a dusty tarp off Mama's snow tires. Using the paint for my presentation, I painted a series of circles in the center of the tarp. White on the outside, followed by yellow, then orange, and finally, a red bull's-eye. I stuffed clothespins in a box, tucked tennis balls into the mermaid cups (they fit perfectly), and nestled them beside my bicycle turbine. And then, using lawn shears, I sliced an empty jug of washer fluid from the top down.

While the paint dried, I packed my newest materials into boxes. And then I dug out a basketball and practiced low dribbles. My fingers were too twitchy to sleep, my heart beating as fast as I bounced the ball, my mind unable to settle down.

13

"When my Santi has a big day, I always make him scrambled eggs, refried beans, and homemade tortillas. Yes, I know it's simple, but sometimes, simple is good," Tía Lucy said, as she presented me my breakfast plate. She adjusted her gold bangles and smoothed her bright orange skirt. Tío Santi probably wore an apron when he cooked; Tía Lucy wore her usual. That morning, it was a floral silk blouse and a tight knee-length skirt. And matching heels, of course.

Mama was on the other side of the kitchen, standing next to Julian, packing up his school bag. Her plate and coffee sat on the table in the spot across from me, steam no longer rising from her beans. Julian was propped up in his chair, his cheek pressed deep into the U-shaped pillow tucked around his neck.

"Do you need anything else?" Tía Lucy asked, her voice as bright as her outfit.

"Just milk, but I'll get it."

I stepped to the fridge to get the milk. The seizure notebook was open on the counter. I peeked at my mother's notes as I poured my milk. It was 7:16 a.m. and the lines were blank. Julian always had a few seizures before breakfast. Papa said they were like morning stretches. Mama hated that comparison. But this morning he hadn't had a single one.

Mama finished packing the bag and began smoothing Julian's hair.

"Inez, you should eat something," Tía Lucy called out.

Mama nodded and sat at the opposite end of the table, leaving Julian across the room, far from me. I watched her fork move around her plate, but she didn't take a bite.

"Isabelle," Tía Lucy said, placing her hand on my arm and slipping into the seat beside me, "what time should we arrive?"

I looked over to Mama. Her eyes were on her plate. They hadn't met mine all morning.

"One o'clock," I said.

Big Betty and Sanchita hopped onto Tía Lucy's lap and sniffed at her plate.

"You better hurry up and eat." Tía Lucy nudged my elbow and I took a bite. Mama picked at her plate while I bit into a tortilla. Abuelito was right: While last night's had tasted like cardboard, this tortilla was delicious.

When I had finished my breakfast, I slipped into my spring jacket, grabbed my gym bag, and pulled on my sandals. Mama helped Julian with his sweatshirt.

Tía Lucy insisted on carrying my science equipment to the car. Mama silently secured Julian in his seat beside me.

"I'll see you in a bit, Isabelle. Have a great day, Julian." Tía Lucy smiled as she held up her Chihuahuas, waving their paws at us until we pulled out of the driveway.

I watched my mother through the rearview as we drove down the street. When she switched on the radio, I leaned over to Julian.

"Hey," I whispered, "I changed our presentation last night."

"Isabelle!" my mother began as she switched the music off. "Leave him be. Let him rest." Now she watched me from the rearview mirror and I straightened in my seat. We traveled the rest of the ride in silence, except for Julian's snores.

Mama dropped me off at school first, as she always did. When she pulled over to the curb, she finally spoke.

"I'm not sure if you noticed, but it is 7:50 in the morning and Julian hasn't had a single seizure."

I turned to Julian. His forehead was pressed against the window. His eyes hadn't opened all morning.

"I noticed," I said, unbuckling from my seat.

"He hasn't had a morning like this in fifteen years, two months, and twelve days, since I started tracking his seizures the day of his diagnosis."

I nodded and placed my hand on Julian's hand.

"It's the new medicine, Isabelle. It's working."

"I know," I said.

Hope rested in her eyes, in her voice.

I kissed Julian on his cheek, grabbed my boxes and bags, and stepped away from the car.

Maybe because I couldn't stop watching the clock, or maybe because the science fair was all anyone was talking about, that morning was the longest I had ever experienced. When the loudspeaker finally called science fair participants down to the cafeteria, I bundled my supplies in my arms and lumbered through the hallway.

I searched the cafeteria tables for my name tag, winding through sections organized by grade level, science genre, and alphabetically by last name. My placement was with the other seventh-grade "Weather and Natural Disaster" projects, in the back, against the wall, sandwiched between a dozen other tables.

I pulled my turbine out of my box, pinned up the tarp three paces away, and angled the jug just so, next to the table leg. I grabbed the fan out of my basket and unwound its cord. On my hands and knees, I crawled under the table and found a nearby outlet. With my tri-fold board up, my report open to the first page, my kneecaps covered in cafeteria crumbs, and my turbine attached, all I needed was Julian.

Julian.

I felt a quiver snake inside my stomach. Between my table and the ones beside it, there wasn't enough room for Julian. Our tables were small and squished together, leaving only a little room for people to pass through. There was no way his wheelchair could fit in beside me, and if it did, it would block the path of anyone wanting to walk by. I shook my head, stood on my tip-toes, and searched for Mrs. Harris. I spotted her propping up a few top-heavy tri-folds.

"Mrs. Harris!" I called out, waving both arms. She looked at me and hurried over.

Pausing for a moment to catch her breath, Mrs. Harris knelt down before my turbine and tarp. Her eyes caught my charts.

"Isabelle," she exclaimed, "this is outstanding. And you engineered this all on your own?"

"I had some inspiration. That's actually what I needed to talk to you about." I stuffed my hands in my pockets, hoping to calm my nerves. "Mrs. Harris, my brother is coming to help me with my experiment. He's going to throw the balls that my turbine collects."

"That sounds great, Isabelle. It's nice that he can help out." She began to step away.

"But, Mrs. Harris, stop!" I spoke up. "There isn't any room for Julian here. Can I switch places to a spot at the end of one of these tables?"

Mrs. Harris looked doubtful, and distracted. The cafeteria was filling up with middle school kids and their voices.

"Isabelle, there isn't time to move. The science fair starts in ten minutes, and everyone is almost finished setting up. You look ready to go. I'll grab a chair from the stage—"

"No." I stepped in front of her to keep her from walking away. "Julian can't sit in one of those chairs. He uses a wheelchair, and there isn't room for him to sit in front of my turbine."

Her eyes broke away from the other students.

"Oh." Mrs. Harris looked at me with kindness and attention. "I didn't know. Let me see what I can do. I'll be back in a moment."

I rolled up my tarp, collapsed my tri-fold, and re-packed my equipment. Seconds later, Mrs. Harris led me to a spot beside the eighth-grade biology and geology projects.

"I'm sorry you won't be with your peers, but there's more room here," she apologized. "I didn't realize your brother would be coming."

"You said siblings could come."

"Yes, I did." Mrs. Harris plugged in my fan and set my tri-fold down at the table. "This spot should work just fine," she said before she scurried off to put paper towels next to the eighth graders' terrariums.

I had just enough time to arrange my display, pin up my tarp, tie my turbine, secure the cardboard blades, and unpack the tennis balls, before I heard a familiar tapping noise grow louder and louder. I looked up to see Tía Lucy and Mama heading toward me. When my eyes found Julian, they teared up. I closed them quickly, so the neighboring eighth graders wouldn't notice.

Julian wasn't smiling. His dimples were lost in droopy cheeks.

"How was Julian's morning?" I asked my mother, looking her over carefully.

"Your brother had a great day at school. No seizures." Mama's smile was guarded as she engaged the brakes on his chair. "I have a feeling that today will be a seizure-free day."

Tía Lucy stepped forward. Her large designer tote pulled at her shoulder as something inside strained against the buckle.

"Isabelle, my darling. This looks magnificent. You should be very proud of yourself."

I blushed as two wet noses peeked out from her bag and sniffed the air.

"Can I move Julian closer?"

Mama hesitated. Tía Lucy nudged her and then my mother nodded.

I pulled Julian's chair beside my turbine, angling it so he faced the tarp with the bull's-eye. I spun the turbine blades and watched the cups climb and fall. I tested a few balls and watched them roll down to the bottom of the tarp, slip into the jug, get scooped up by a cup, ride up the pulley, and tumble onto Julian's tray. Everything was in working order.

Except Julian.

I leaned close to his ear.

"Julian," I whispered. "Julian, can you hear me? Could you wake up? Can you try?"

His breathing stayed the same. It didn't deepen. He didn't shift. I placed my hand on his arm. My hand slipped into his and I gave him a squeeze.

"Julian." I took a deep breath and looked up. "Mama?"

"Yes, Isabelle." Her eyes darted to Julian, and then her shoulders relaxed when she saw his sleeping face.

"Was Julian sleeping all day?" I tried to keep my voice flat, but she grew stiff anyway.

"It's a side effect. You know that," she said.

"What's wrong, Isabelle?" Tía Lucy stepped over.

"Julian's a part of my demonstration. He is supposed to throw the tennis balls and my turbine will collect them. But he's asleep. He's always asleep."

Mama opened her mouth to say something as the lights dimmed.

"Good morning," my principal called out on a megaphone, her voice swelling the way only a middle school principal's voice can swell. "Welcome, families, to the tenth annual seventh- and eighth-grade McKinley School Science Fair! Please ask a lot of questions. Our junior scientists have worked very hard, and are eager to teach you what they've learned. When you finish, place your vote for the best presentation in the basket beside the podium. Science teachers will vote on one seventh-grade finalist and one eighth-grade finalist. The audience-choice finalist can be from either grade level."

I squatted next to Julian's chair. I massaged his hand. I sang Papa's silly morning song in his ear.

"Good morning, morning, morning. Good morning, Julian."

His eyelashes twitched. I deepened my voice to make it sound more like Papa's.

"The sun is up, yellow like a duck."

His head pulled away from me, fighting to stay asleep.

"Ducks that quack . . ."

"Isabelle, what on earth are you singing?" Tía Lucy whispered, stifling a shudder.

"It's a song Papa sings to us. I'm trying to wake Julian up."

She looked over at Mama, then to the neighboring students before scooping Sanchita out of her bag. She moved Sanchita close to Julian's face. Soon, he was covered in Chihuahua kisses. That did the trick. Julian's right eye pulled open and the left one soon followed.

"Inez, come with me. It might be easier for Isabelle to get started if she has a little space." Tía Lucy slipped her arm through my mother's and led her away before my mother could object. But Mama turned around, shooting me one last look. Goose bumps climbed up my arms. I rubbed them off.

"Okay, Julian." I stooped down and looked directly at him. His eyes were open, but kept threatening to close. His head swiveled on his neck. He pulled his arms close to his chest. And then, he smiled.

"Let's do this," I said.

I switched on my table fan and watched my turbine come to life. Julian's right hand crawled across his tray. I poured my tube of tennis balls onto the tarp. They rolled down the slope and lined up, awaiting the cups from the turbine.

A few parents and a group of sixth graders gathered around.

"Welcome to my presentation on wind energy. My hand-crafted turbine uses wind power to deposit these tennis balls up onto my brother's tray."

My audience ducked down to watch a tennis ball ride up inside its mermaid cup. The turbine spun and the belt moved smoothly. When Julian's fingers found the first tennis ball, his smile grew large. He pulled his arm back and threw the ball at the bull's-eye.

Thud!

The ball hit the yellow ring, fell to the tarp, and rolled back in line with the other balls. Applause rang in my ears.

The next ball rolled onto Julian's tray. His left hand found it and slowly brought the ball over to his right hand. The transfer was clumsy. I looked up at Julian's face. His eyes were closing.

"Julian, you can do this," I whispered.

He blinked a few times, pulled his arm back, and threw the ball.

Smack!

He hit the orange ring.

"Nice job, Julian!" I patted his arm. "You got closer to the center this time." I turned to the growing crowd. "For this display, I'm using an electric fan. But my turbine is designed to use

the wind to power its movement. It currently serves two additional purposes: popcorn dispenser"—I held up a photo of Papa
awaiting a serving of popcorn—"and a paint machine." I lifted
the second belt with the attached paintbrushes and a sketch of
how the turbine would operate.

The audience smiled as I turned to Julian.

The third ball was on his tray. The ball kept slipping from
his hand. The fourth ball was nearing the top of the belt. When
he finally had the ball in his grip, he pulled his arm back and it
tumbled out. I bent down and picked it up.

"That's okay." I held his hand and tucked the ball into his palm.

The fourth ball rolled across his tray and the fifth ball slipped
into its cup.

"You can do it, Julian. No rush."

He looked up at me, his foggy eyes half hidden by droopy
lids. His deep brown eyes held mine. They creased in the corners. And then they opened wide. Too wide.

That's when it happened.

Julian's eyes rolled back, and his head jerked to the side. His
arms retracted. The tennis ball stayed tight in his fist—for a
moment—and then it popped out and tumbled to the ground.

In that instant, my brain switched from presenter to protec-
tor. I stepped to Julian's chair, knelt down, and whispered into
his ear: "Cálmate. I'm here with you."

One second.

"You're okay. Julian, can you hear me? Don't worry."

Two seconds.

"I'm with you. Cálmate. It's okay."

Three seconds.

My heart wasn't pounding; it was trying to escape. My ribs felt bruised and beaten as they kept it prisoner.

Four seconds.

His arms shook, his legs trembled.

Five seconds.

"Julian!" A voice shrieked. Mama's voice.

Six seconds.

His body jerked against his chair. Julian's beautiful, black eyelashes fluttered.

Seven seconds.

Julian exhaled deeply and then his muscles relaxed. His head rolled on his shoulders into my awaiting hands. I gently leaned him back into his headrest. I pressed my lips against his forehead and said one last: "It's okay. I'm here."

Mama rushed over and squeezed between the two of us, knocking tennis balls off his tray and onto the floor where they bounced against my feet and under the tables.

"Isabelle! What happened?" she scolded. Her face was more anguished than it had been on the morning of the big seizure. Her eyes were wide and wild, her lips pale and thin.

"Julian had a seizure."

"Yes, but what did you do to him?"

"Nothing, Mama." I shook my head. "I didn't do anything."

"I knew he shouldn't have come," she muttered, brushing her hand along Julian's cheek.

"Excuse me." A father stepped from my crowd. "Should we call an ambulance?"

"No," Mama said.

I looked up at the man, whose eyes moved between Mama and Julian.

"It's okay," I said. "Julian has a kind of epilepsy. He has seizures all the time."

"I'll go get the nurse," he insisted, and rushed off before we could object.

Mama stood up slowly and released the brakes on Julian's chair.

"We're leaving, Isabelle."

"But, Mama." I took a deep breath to calm my trembling. "It was just one seizure. He's my assistant—and my inspiration. I want him to stay."

"Isabelle, this isn't about what *you* want. Don't you understand? Julian almost had an entire day free of seizures. He's had no seizures all morning. It was a mistake to leave him with you. Just ten minutes in your care and he has a seizure. It was so . . . so careless."

Someone coughed. Mama closed her eyes and inhaled.

I wiped away my tears, leaned forward, and nuzzled my nose against the top of Julian's head.

"Mama's taking you home to rest," I whispered. "Thanks for all of your help. I'll see you after my basketball practice."

"Pardon me," Mama said to the students and parents, pushing Julian's chair away from me. As she inched forward, Julian's left arm fell to the side of his chair. He reached out and his hand found mine. His fingers laced between my fingers, forming a tangled knot.

Mama turned and looked at me, and then down at our hands. Julian pulled his head up. It took great effort and a few tries. His eyes slowly opened, first the right, then the left. Julian's right hand turned over on his tray. His fingers uncurled like a blooming flower.

"*Yip!*" Sanchita had appeared at my ankles, her tiny teeth gripping the fuzz at the top of a tennis ball. I snatched Sanchita and draped her across my shoulders. I pressed the tennis ball into Julian's hand.

And that's when I noticed that my audience had grown bigger. They were watching Julian; they were watching me.

"Julian wants to stay," I said.

"He needs to rest," Mama said firmly.

"Please, Mama?" I asked.

She gave me a long look. Finally, reluctantly, Mama's hands released from his chair.

I stepped forward and brought Julian back beside my turbine.

Julian pulled his hand back slowly. His arm quivered with effort. When he released the ball, it tumbled just past his chair, far from the bull's-eye, but the applause was louder than before. Mama turned to the crowd, her cheeks pink.

The crowd watched the next tennis ball roll down the tarp, into a cup, and climb up the belt. Julian's left hand squeezed mine as his right waited for the ball. I cleared my throat, looked out to my mother, and then to our audience.

"I studied wind because of Julian. He loves it. He loves the way it feels. He loves watching the wind instruments in our yard.

"I designed this turbine to do other things, but I changed it last night so Julian could play with his tennis balls on his own, without needing help from anyone else. I don't mind giving him a hand, but it's also important for Julian to have opportunities to do things on his own. He can do so much, but with tools like this, he can do even more."

I watched Julian. I watched the creases at the corner of his eyes deepen as the next tennis ball left his fingertips. I witnessed his black hair fluttering backwards—like the frill of a cockatoo—from the draft of the fan. Each time his head drooped to his shoulder, he pulled it back. He fought the fatigue, which trailed his every move. I looked at my mother, and at the parents, students, and teachers who had crowded in closer to the turbine.

When the ball finally hit the bull's-eye in the center, Julian ran out of energy. His right hand fell limp on the tray. But his smile remained long after his eyes had closed and his snores had settled into a steady rhythm.

There was applause, gentle applause. A few parents gave me a thumbs-up. Others patted Julian's arm.

"Isabelle! Sorry we were held up."

Mrs. Harris rushed forward through the crowd with the school nurse at her side. She placed her hand gently on my shoulder. "There were some critter escapes in the biology section. We heard your brother had a seizure!"

"It's okay," I said, looking over to my mother who stood silently beside us. "He gets them all the time."

"Are you sure?" Mrs. Harris asked.

"Yes," I said.

Tía Lucy came rushing in behind them, her eyes opened too

wide, like an owl at dusk.

"I tried to come as soon as I could, but some poor boy's ant farm cracked and I didn't want to flatten his ants with my heels, and then there was a snake escape on the other end of the cafeteria . . . " Tía Lucy's hand rested on my mother's shoulder. Mama turned her head away. "Inez, what's going on?"

"Julian had a seven-second seizure," Mama said, letting a sob escape.

"Isabelle?" Tía Lucy turned to me.

"Julian got a bull's-eye. I'm serious. He got it all on his own. You should have seen it. He was so happy."

"We were so close." Mama turned to Tía Lucy. "So close to a day without—"

"Smiling?" I interrupted.

Mama pulled a tissue out from her pocket. She wouldn't look at me.

I continued. "He was *smiling*, Tía Lucy. He got those wrinkles next to his eyes. You know those wrinkles? He was smiling because he tried again and again to get the bull's-eye. And he finally did."

Tía Lucy's eyebrows crept to the top of her forehead. She looked over at my mother, at Julian, and then back at me.

"Julian fell asleep with a smile on his face. It's gone now, but his left dimple was so big."

Mama shook her head as she stepped closer to Julian's chair. "Isabelle," she said, sadness pulling at her eyes. "He was so close— don't you see?"

"Yes, Mama." I nodded. "He had one seizure so far today,

and maybe he could have had none."

"Isabelle, I don't think you understand what we'd give up if we stopped this new medicine."

I thought of my nights with Julian in Las Brisas, swimming together in the ocean, playing basketball, talking. If things changed, I might never go back there.

"You're wrong, Mama. I know what we're giving up. We're giving up what I've always wanted . . . but it's not enough. We need to think about Julian."

She shook her head and smiled. It was a sad smile. A small, sad smile.

"But Mama"—she held up a hand to stop me from speaking, but I continued anyway—"Julian almost had a day without smiling. Without playing, without laughing. Without having fun. He threw a bull's-eye!"

"You're not listening, Isabelle. The doctors are treating his seizures." She sighed deeply. "This is the next course if we want to try to be rid of them forever."

"Excuse me," Tía Lucy interrupted, peeking inside her purse and then up at my shoulders. "How did Sanchita get here?"

"I don't know," I said, stroking her chin. "She came by after the seizure and brought me a tennis ball."

Big Betty tried to squirm her way out of the bag, but her belly couldn't get past the clasp.

"Inez." Tía Lucy stepped closer. "You can discuss this later. Let's walk around a bit more, so Isabelle can continue her presentation without us taking up all her space. We seem to be scaring away observers."

Mama reached for his wheelchair. "But Julian is—"

"Julian is sleeping. What's there to worry about?"

Once again, Tía Lucy lured my mother away. This time, I presented my turbine without Julian's assistance. I showcased my design plans. Audience members threw tennis balls and high-fived when they hit the bull's-eye. I never once let go of Julian's hand.

With five minutes left in the school day, my principal dimmed the lights and stood at the podium.

"Attention, scientists and guests! I am now closing the votes. Your teachers will quickly count the ballots and, in a moment, I will announce the audience-choice award winner for the science fair. In the meantime, I would like to congratulate Peter Beaulieu for winning the eighth-grade award, for his detailed research on the history of vaccines. And for the seventh grade, Eloise Williams has been awarded the prize for her research on snail fossils."

My principal pushed the microphone away as she consulted with the science teachers.

Tía Lucy and my mother returned. Mama stood on the other side of Julian, Big Betty tucked in the crook of her arm as she absently scratched her ears.

The principal pulled the microphone close again and tapped it a couple of times.

"May I have your attention, please? Now for the audience-choice award. This vote is usually a tight race, but not this year. It is my honor to congratulate Isabelle Perez for earning nearly two hundred audience votes for her detailed research and her incredible wind turbine."

She paused as applause filled the cafeteria.

"Isabelle chose to engineer a project which opens up possibilities. She will join Peter and Eloise at the Regional Science Showcase in two weeks."

"Did you hear that, Julian?" I knelt down beside him. "Julian, I'm going to Regionals! We did it!"

"Congratulations, Isabelle!" Tía Lucy pulled me in for a tight hug. Sanchita licked my arm.

My mother, still on the other side of Julian, wiped her eyes.

"Inez . . ." Tía Lucy began.

"I thought it was going to be a great day for Julian."

I looked over at my mother. The back of my throat burned and my nose began to run.

"Inez, shame on you. It *is* a great day." Tía Lucy pursed her bright red lips. "Your daughter has won a prize for all of her hard work, and your son threw a bull's-eye. And if it's only seizures you care about, Julian has had just one."

Mama reached for the wheelchair.

"Come on, Julian." She pulled his chair away and I let his fingers slip out of mine.

Tía Lucy stepped over and kissed me on my cheeks. "I'll have a word with her. Don't get yourself down, okay?"

I nodded and wiped my nose on my sleeve.

"Isabelle?"

"Yes?" I blinked away my tears and looked over at her big brown eyes.

"How are you able to see all that's possible?"

I shrugged.

"This is your gift, Isabelle. But not everyone sees what you see. Remember my visit last year? You opened my eyes." Tía Lucy looked over her shoulder. "I'd better run, or your mother might leave without me. It'll be okay, Isabelle."

"Will it?"

"Yes, my darling niece." Tía Lucy pulled me in for another tight hug filled with wet Chihuahua kisses. "It will."

14

After school, I walked to the Y for my basketball practice. The middle school season was over, but I played on a club team at the Y with a lot of the same girls. The routine was identical week after week. We dribbled up the court and back, first with our right hands, then with our left. Half of our team practiced layups while the other half alternated between rebounding and squats. Next, Coach taught us picks and pass moves for the upcoming game. When we were limber, sweaty, and tired of drills, it was scrimmage time. With five minutes left in practice, Coach blew his whistle, and it was time for free throws.

I loved free throws. They were dependable, consistent, and safe. Standing at the line, I dribbled three times and balanced the ball in my hand—using only my fingertips, just like Coach had taught me. With the ball resting on the pads of my fingertips, I took a deep breath, crouched down, and aimed. I always ended with my follow-through. *Icing on the cake* is what Coach called it. I didn't have to watch the ball to know it was going through. I never missed my free throws.

"Nice shot, Isabelle," Coach said.

I nodded and returned to the end of the line.

"You were so brave today," Anna leaned back and whispered.

"I wasn't brave," I said.

"Yes, you were." She leaned in closer. "I heard that you helped your brother during his seizure. That's very brave of you."

"No, I wasn't brave," I repeated. "I was just doing what I was taught to do. It's how I help Julian when he's seizing."

"I think I would have been scared. Or maybe frozen still," she said.

We inched forward as each girl took a turn.

"Congratulations on your award."

"Thanks." I smiled.

"Hey, Anna," Coach called out. "You're next. Get ready."

Anna spun around just as Coach passed the ball.

"All right, Anna. Remember what we talked about last time. Follow through. It's like—"

"Icing on the cake," she finished for Coach.

Anna dribbled the ball, crouched, aimed, and let go. The ball bounced around the rim and fell off the side.

"Close, Anna. Bend your knees more next time."

When Coach looked over and saw that I was in front of the line, his eyes brightened.

"Isabelle, keep doing what you're doing."

I dribbled three times. I turned to the bleachers and imagined Julian was there, watching me play. I pictured his eyes. And for a split second, I heard his voice cheering me on—not his Las Brisas voice, just his everyday voice.

Taking a deep breath, I released the ball. The basketball left my fingertips and floated up in the air. It arched and fell, sliding perfectly through the hoop.

"Excellent, Isabelle. Great shot," Coach called out.

"Thanks," I said.

As I walked back to the line, I heard some faint applause.

"You've got a fan club," Anna whispered.

I looked out across the bleachers. The usual faces were there: moms and dads, some younger brothers and sisters. And then I saw him, standing stooped by the door. His dark eyes staring into mine.

"Abuelito?"

"Who?" Anna asked.

"It's my *abuelo*, my grandfather."

Abuelito stood so still, like an Aztec statue carved out of stone.

"Ladies, it's time for our huddle." Coach blew his whistle and waved us in. He ended every practice with a huddle.

"Big game Sunday. Remember to practice your picks and rolls. Get your hand on a basketball, dribble and shoot for at least thirty minutes each day." He looked everyone in the eyes and then finished, "See you in two days."

We threw our hands in the middle and yelled: "Go Blue!"

I quickly changed out of my basketball sneakers and walked over to Abuelito.

"Hi, Isabelle. I'm here to give you a ride home."

"You are?"

"I am," he said. "You made all your baskets."

"I always do," I said softly.

We stood in silence as my teammates walked past. The silence deepened and I remembered Tía Lucy's story about Abuelito's magic hands, the soft scars buried deep inside his palm. I pulled my shoulders back.

"Maybe I have hands like yours," I offered.

"No," he said.

My cheeks grew hot. I squared my shoulders.

"I watched you, Isabelle. The way you dribble the ball, the way it leaves your fingers . . ." Abuelito reached for my hand. Tía Lucy was right; the inside of his hand was incredibly soft and warm. My hand didn't stay nestled inside his for long. Abuelito uncurled my fingers. He inspected my dusty fingerprints and the lines in my palms. Then, with great effort, he closed his hand around mine. "You have your own hands, Isabelle, and they are magic. I am sorry I didn't celebrate them sooner."

"Gracias," I whispered.

Abuelito didn't let go of my hand when he wrapped his arm around my shoulders and pulled me into a hug.

"I've wasted so many years," he said, his stubbly cheek brushing against my forehead.

"Well, you're here now," I said.

Abuelito took hold of both my hands, lining his palms up against mine. His eighty-two-year-old hand was the same size as my twelve-year-old one. I squeezed his hand and he squeezed mine back.

"I won the audience-choice award today, at my science fair."

"You did?"

I nodded.

"Yes. For my research, and for the wind turbine I made. I get to compete again in two weeks, at Regionals."

"Will you show me your machine?"

"Maybe you can come see it at Regionals."

"I'd like that."

We walked to Abuelito's car. The leather seats were worn and cracked. My thighs squeaked and burned as I slid across the cushions.

I hadn't ridden in Abuelito's car since Abuelita had passed away, many years ago. The car still smelled like lilies, cinnamon, and orange.

"Did you know that Julian's going to play in an orchestra?" I asked as I buckled my seat belt.

"What was that?" Abuelito turned in his seat. Up close, his profile was striking.

I leaned in closer and raised my voice. "Julian is playing in an orchestra."

"That's interesting." Abuelito nodded to himself.

"He's going to play the tambourine," I continued, waiting to see how Abuelito would respond. He paused and swallowed.

"Will there be a concert?" he asked, holding his keys in his hand.

"I don't know." I stopped to consider it. "But probably, since it's an orchestra."

He cleared his throat. "Well, I guess it's a good time to get my hearing aid adjusted."

Abuelito turned back around, his fingers wrestling with the car key as he tried to insert it in the ignition. The key ring slipped between his fingers and fell to the floor. He grunted, reached down, and fished around for the keys. Once they were in his hands again, he worked to separate the car key from the others, but they kept slipping.

"Let me help," I said, unbuckling my seat belt and leaning forward.

Abuelito sighed and handed me the keys. I pulled the car key from the rest of the bunch and held it out for Abuelito. His fingers carefully pulled it from my grasp—like he was selecting the most delicate rose from a bouquet.

"Gracias, Isabelle," Abuelito said as he started the car.

"*De nada*," I said. "Anytime."

"Why are you home so early?" I asked, pulling my backpack off my shoulders and dropping my gym bag on the floor.

"Hello to you, Isabelle! And hello, Abuelito." Papa grinned at me and nodded at Abuelito. "I'd swapped shifts so I'd be busy next week when Lucia was supposed to visit. So now, I'm off for the next few days, and we get to spend quality time together. Lucia is thrilled."

I stepped out of my shoes and peeled off my socks.

"Did Mama tell you about my award?"

Papa's smile grew larger.

"You bet she did. Congratulations, *mija*." Papa scooped my ball out of my arms and pulled me into a tight hug. "I'm so proud of you."

"Papá! I know you're here," Tía Lucy's voice called out. "Come to the kitchen for some coffee."

Abuelito nodded to Papa and shuffled toward my tía's voice.

"He surprised me at practice," I said.

"I think your tía had something to do with it." Papa's arms slipped from the hug and he stuffed them into his pockets. "Your mother and I have done a lot of talking. We've got some decisions to make, Isabelle. They won't be easy."

"Are you talking about Julian's medicine?"

"I am."

"Does this mean that Mama's not mad at me anymore?"

Papa nodded.

As I stepped into the kitchen, Mama met me with a long, tight hug. Julian sat in his chair beside my seat. His smile was delicious.

"Julian's doctor can't change much right away, but we can take away his dinnertime meds and delay his bedtime ones." She sat down across from me. Her smile was relaxed; her hand held Abuelito's. "We're going to have more appointments, and Isabelle, I'll try to schedule them after school so you can come, too."

Tía Lucy placed a tray of mole enchiladas in the center of the table, snatching Papa's fork from his fingers.

"Now, before you dig into these enchiladas, I want you to pay attention to your tongues as they find the different spices. It took Santi and me eleven months to perfect—"

The microwave beeped.

"I must have forgotten something," Tía Lucy said as she scooted from the table and opened the door. "Huh, that's odd; it's empty."

Julian chuckled beside me. Once Tía Lucy sat down, he started up again. Tía Lucy leapt to her feet but paused when she reached the microwave. By then, Julian was laughing so hard he snorted and his toys tumbled off his tray.

"Julian! Sinvergüenza!" Tía Lucy scolded, though she couldn't help but smile.

Julian seized just moments later. Mama turned to soothe him, Abuelito watched, while I counted. When the seizure was over, Mama looked up at me.

"Isabelle, why don't you mark it?"

I nodded. "Ten seconds." I pushed out of my seat and walked to the counter where the notebook was kept. When I marked it on the fourth line in the notebook, I noticed that there was a new column on the page.

"What's this?" I asked. Mama walked over and wrapped her arm around my shoulder.

"I added a new column so that I'll remember to take note of the good things that Julian does during the day." She pointed to the lines already filled.

Threw a bull's-eye during the science fair. Practiced tambourine for 20 minutes.

"How about you add: *Tricked the Taco Queen?*" Papa suggested.

"How about you can go without your slice of my flourless chocolate cake?" Tía Lucy asked, her eyebrow arching dramatically. Papa's face drooped. Her chocolate cake was Papa's favorite, though he hated to admit it.

While we ate the enchiladas, Mama and Tía Lucy discussed their favorite science fair exhibits and Abuelito described my jump shot. With our bellies almost full, Tía Lucy served dessert. Papa ate two helpings.

Julian's yawns were soon too large to ignore. Abuelito kissed him good night, Mama gave him his meds, and Papa carried him to bed.

"Go on to bed, Isabelle," Mama said as she tucked Julian in. "You've had quite a day. You must be tired."

"Mama?"

"Yes, dear?"

Her large brown eyes looked up at me. They smiled from their corners, giving me courage.

"Can I sleep in Julian's room tonight?" I asked.

Her fingers knotted together. She looked over at Julian and then back at me.

"You don't want to sleep upstairs with Tía Lucy?" she asked.

"Can you blame her?" Tía Lucy popped her head in from the kitchen, giving me a subtle wink. "Big Betty has some congestion and her snores are something else. I've tried some of Santi's nasal strips on her, but they don't work so well on Chihuahua noses."

"Big surprise," Papa muttered.

Mama looked at me and shrugged.

"Why not?" She stood and kissed my forehead. "Say good night to your grandfather, and then go get your things."

Abuelito stood by the door, a plastic tub of leftover enchiladas in one hand, a container filled with flourless chocolate cake in the other. Papa looked on with envy.

"Good night," I said as my arms reached out for a hug. "Thanks for coming to my practice."

"Good night, Isabelle. Thank you . . . for everything."

15

That night was the first in a long time when I didn't count down until bedtime. I wasn't waiting for the darkness to deepen. I didn't listen for silence to settle. I was already with Julian.

Branches tapped against his windows. A few cars swooshed by.

Julian's hospital balloons drooped on their strings. Shriveled and puckered, they were still afloat—barely. My fingers traced the metal footboard of Julian's bed. I watched his quilt slowly rise with each breath. Footsteps shuffled upstairs. Papa and Tía Lucy were laughing about something. I strained to hear, but their words were too far away. Mama's voice joined in, followed by sharp Chihuahua barks. My lips parted in a smile. Doors pushed closed, floorboards creaked and eased. And then silence.

I stood beside Julian, whose breathing was steady and deep. I tucked my basketball trophy under his left arm and smoothed his quilt. And then I walked over to the dresser.

The pinwheel was still and Julian's room smelled like mole enchiladas. I pulled open the bottom drawer and took out one of his sweatshirts. I slipped it on over my head and rolled up the cuffs. It smelled like Julian, warm and welcoming.

Standing on my tiptoes, I looked at the corkboard above his dresser where a collage of photos was arranged—Julian's first day at his school, the two of us flying kites in the field next to my school. My favorite was a photo of us from the Halloween when Julian had dressed up like an ice-cream truck, and I had been an ice-cream cone.

I sat in Mama's chair and leaned my pillow against the side of Julian's bed. As my fingers slipped in between his, my eyes closed.

I woke up some time later. My neck was stiff. My fingers tingled. I looked for the pinwheel but couldn't see it. Darkness had crept into Julian's room. Shadows curled around the furniture. I watched them slip from the moon as it journeyed through the sky.

"I'm okay with this," I whispered. With each heartbeat, my grip tightened. "It's okay, because we have tomorrow, Julian. Dr. Holland will ease you off those meds, so you'll be tired, but not as tired. We can practice your tambourine."

I closed my eyes and let out a breath.

"I just thought I'd have a little more time with you in Las Brisas."

Sleep did not come. Though every inch of me was tired, my hand would not release Julian's. And then finally, in the early hours of the morning, when birds chirped to greet the sun before it crested the horizon, I smelled oranges—oranges warmed in the California sunshine.

"Belle!" Julian called out. "Are you here?"

I turned to him. His deep brown eyes opened wide, waiting for an answer.

"Always," I said. "I brought you something."

Julian looked over at his other hand.

"Your trophy."

"I dug it out of my closet for you."

"Promise me you won't hide it anymore."

"I promise," I said.

"Your eyes are smiling," Julian whispered.

"I know," I said. "I'm not worried anymore."

Julian slid off his bed and we sat together on the floor. I leaned into him and Julian wrapped his arms around me.

"Julian," I whispered. "What if we just stay and talk? What if we don't go to Las Brisas?"

"It doesn't work like that," Julian said. "If you don't go to Las Brisas, everything returns to normal."

"Like Cinderella at midnight."

"Yeah." Julian smiled. "Belle, do you remember the time Mama found me on the floor? When she thought I'd rolled out of bed?"

Boy, did I remember that morning. Mama's shriek had sliced through the house. It was a miracle the neighbors hadn't come running. I had flown down the stairs to find Mama stooped next to Julian, who was laying half in the kitchen and half in his room.

Once it was clear he wasn't injured, Mama and I had lifted Julian and placed him in his wheelchair. For the rest of the day, Mama took on the role of a crime scene detective. She reenacted all of the possible ways Julian—who could move his arms and legs a little, but had never been able to support his own weight—had managed to land eight feet from his bed. She measured and re-measured using a yardstick. She practiced falling out of his bed multiple times. In the end, Mama declared it a mystery, never to be spoken of again.

The stillness in Julian's room tightened. I took slow breaths and felt Julian's pulse beating in his hand.

Julian's head leaned against mine.

And then the ceiling trembled.

Julian and I stood and watched as the top of our house lifted off. It tore free as though a giant's hand had pulled it apart with one swift motion. The walls fell away and Las Brisas swept in.

A ripple of fuchsia clouds swirled down from above. They spun in spirals. Once they'd finished dancing, they settled like down feathers and warmed the horizon.

We walked toward them.

The ground sloped upward and Julian pulled me along. We climbed up and up and up. My legs burned, but Julian marched on. When we finally reached the crest of the hill, I spotted a quilt on the ground—Julian's quilt. And I suddenly knew where we were: the hill behind the high school, where we watched the Fourth of July fireworks every year. On top of the quilt lay a red-laced baseball tucked inside a baseball glove.

Julian slipped his hand out from mine, bent down, and slid the glove onto his hand.

"Do you want to play catch?" Julian asked. He tossed me the baseball before I could answer.

Julian stepped to the other side of the quilt, balled up his right hand, and smacked it into the brown leather glove.

I took a few steps back, careful not to tumble down the hill.

Julian leaned forward and bent his knees. Taking a deep breath, I threw the ball. It went a little to the side, but Julian caught it effortlessly.

"Oops," I muttered. "I'm not used to throwing a baseball."

"No worries." Julian lobbed the ball back to me. "Be sure to follow through. *Icing on the cake*, right? And use your whole body, not just your arm."

I tried it again. I bent my knees, swung my arm back, and threw the ball. This time it slapped Julian's glove when he caught it.

"Nice!" Julian said, tossing the ball back to me.

My fingertips felt along the baseball, feeling the stitches and the coolness of the leather. As I prepared my next throw, my eyes lingered on Julian's glove. It didn't look like the baseball gloves from gym class. The color was richer. It looked like a fat, leather garden glove.

"Julian?"

"Yeah?"

"Where did you get that glove?"

Julian straightened from his crouch and held it up.

"From Abuelito."

"Abuelito?" The baseball fell from my hand.

"Yeah." Julian stepped closer. He slid the glove off his hand and passed it to me. The palm was a deep brown, soft and stained from catching hundreds of baseballs. I slid my hand inside. The leather was heavy and smelled like summer nights. Every wrinkle in the glove told a story.

"Abuelito gave this to you?" I asked, slipping it off and handing it back to Julian.

Julian shook his head and smiled.

"No. Not yet. But one day he will."

"You think so?"

Julian nodded.

I took a few steps back, picked up the ball, and prepared to pitch it again.

We played catch until it got too dark to see. When the pink clouds faded and the sky deepened to the color of hot coffee, Julian and I stretched out on his quilt, watching stars pierce the darkness with their blades of silver.

"Look, Belle! The Big Dipper!"

My eyes searched the sky. I spotted the four stars of the Dipper's cup and followed the three on the handle.

A cool breeze brushed over us, carrying in the smell of fresh-cut grass and early summer nights. A cricket chirped somewhere close by. Lightning bugs danced and darted in and out of our view. Shooting stars swooped overhead. A few more stars twinkled.

I swept my hand on top of the grass, letting it tickle my palm.

"I'll miss sharing Las Brisas with you," Julian whispered.

"Me, too." I searched the sadness in his face. My heart pounded and my cheeks grew hot. I wiped my eyes. "You've got an orchestra to prepare for. We should practice tomorrow, first thing."

Julian nodded.

We lay in silence a little longer. Julian broke it first.

"I had fun fooling with Tía Lucy at dinner."

"I'd told her about that trick, and she still didn't realize."

"It's because I'm that good at it." Julian wiggled his eyebrows and I laughed.

I swallowed hard and looked up at the sky, to the stars sparkling all around me.

"I love you, Belle."

"I love you, too."

Crickets creaked quiet notes. The stars shimmered softly. Lightning bugs hovered in midair.

"Julian?" My hand slipped into his.

"Yes?"

"Maybe I can make cards with pictures of places we've visited, and, I don't know, some categories for new places you could go to. And then I can ask you about Las Brisas. It would take some time to get it right, but we could figure it out."

"That's a great idea." Julian smiled.

I looked out over the hillside as darkness drifted toward us. Time was running out.

The grass grew damp with dew. The stars brightened and clustered. I focused on the warmth of Julian's hand, the softness of his breath. The happiness in my heart. I took a deep breath, and then sat up and gasped.

"What is it, Belle?"

I saw it. A vision in the stars.

I saw the cenote. Julian sharing a kayak with Papa. Mama swimming beside me. I saw a stadium filled with people. The smell of sweat, the sound of sneakers squeaking on waxed wood. The halftime buzzer, Julian waving to me from the crowd. I saw a coral reef and beautiful fish circling a weightless wheelchair with a scuba tank attached.

The scenes kept changing, flashing, flickering. In them I saw sunsets and sidewalks, moon glow and mountaintops.

And Julian.

I saw Julian skiing snowy trails in a modified wheelchair. I heard his voice spoken through a computer. I saw his warm smiles and his deep brown eyes.

"What is it, Belle?" Julian asked again.

"It's nothing," I said.

But it was everything.

Epilogue

It begins as a hint, as soft as a good-night kiss, notes lifting into the air, whispers.

The tremor moves from Julian's hand to his arm to his chest. Growing stronger still, like wind threading through fresh green leaves, pushing against branches, boughs bending and swaying until the whole tree is alive and dancing.

The grand performance of Julian's orchestra has just begun.

Mama's arm tightens around my shoulders. She gives me a squeeze. Her eyes don't leave Julian, but she holds me tight and won't let go. Papa's on the other side. His hand slips around mine.

Suddenly, Mrs. Pemberly's foot pounds the stage floor. She stomps again and again. Her hands whirl through the air, fingers snapping. The chime of Julian's tambourine catches her rhythm. Dylan presses his lips against his recorder and lets out a note, like wind driving into a keyhole. It is long and strong. It arches higher as the ring in Julian's tambourine drizzles down.

Sylvia comes in on her bongo. Her hands are stronger than Mrs. Pemberly's feet. Sylvia's fingers tap-dance along the rim, her palm sending beats into our bodies. *Ba-bom, ba-bom, ba-bom-bom-bom.*

Mrs. Pemberly shuffles and sways to the edge of the stage as Julian's orchestra takes flight. They play together. They take turns. Solos become duets. They blend, they contrast, they create energy. They finish in a frenzy of beats and notes too chaotic to catch, but perfect in every way.

Jamie and her high school friends dance in the aisle. Anna's eye catches mine and she gives me a thumbs-up. When the music finally stops, Julian, Dylan, and Sylvia bow their heads. I clap so hard that my palms turn pink, but Abuelito claps the loudest.

"Bravo, Julian!" Tía Lucy shouts as the crowd calls for an encore. The Chihuahuas bark.

Onstage, Julian wipes his brow. His eyes find mine and his smile deepens. His smile is so much like Papa's.

Mrs. Pemberly walks to the center of the stage. The sequins in her skirt send rainbows of light across the audience.

"My musicians now invite you, their family and friends, to join us onstage. For our encore, please choose an instrument." Mrs. Pemberly gestures to the baskets placed around the stage.

The girls on my basketball team grab egg shakers. Coach's fingers fiddle with a ukulele. Papa grabs some spoons; Mama hands Abuelito a rain stick as she pulls out a xylophone. Tía Lucy reaches for a cowbell. Dr. Holland has a cymbal in each hand.

I make my way over to Julian. He slides his maraca out of his backpack and into my hands.

We hear the stomp of Mrs. Pemberly's foot and stand at attention. When she stomps the floor again, Julian, Sylvia, and Dylan begin a new song. The audience joins in, slowly at first, mirroring their beats until we've warmed up.

And then the music takes over. It pulses, it grows. There are no words to their songs, but I hear them in Dylan's melody, in Julian and Sylvia's rhythm: strength, resilience, and love. I miss Las Brisas, but this—this is better.

Acknowledgments

A big thank you goes to Beth Brogna, for mentoring me in the teaching of writing. You encouraged me to look beyond the script and, instead, expand my students' craft with writer's tools, strong leads, and slowed-down time. Your lessons not only improved my teaching, you rekindled my love of writing.

I have endless gratitude for the time Siobhan Foley and Liza Halley spent reading my rough drafts, revised drafts, and rough revised drafts. Your thoughtful and honest feedback over these past few years was invaluable.

My mother, Yolanda Aliberti, is always willing to read through drafts, even with tight deadlines. Thank you.

I also need to thank my Lewiston public school teachers, who taught me to read and write, and who inspired me to love reading and writing. My Mount Holyoke College professors, thank you for honing my craft.

My editor, Melissa Kim, saw the possibilities in my submission—a draft which transformed and blossomed over many revisions. With your special gift, you guided me each step of the way. Thank you to Dean Lunt and everyone at Islandport Press, for your edits, insights, and the amazing cover. Thank you for believing in my book.

I am grateful that my three children, Sol, Cortez, and Frida, and my husband, Aaron, give me time and space to write—something my cats don't seem to understand.

And most of all, thank you, Mateo, for those Sunday morning snuggles.

About the Author

Sarah Marie Aliberti Jette grew up in Lewiston, Maine, in a house filled with books. A graduate of Mount Holyoke College, she served in the Peace Corps in Mongolia, studied rehabilitation counseling, and now has the best job in the world: teaching fourth-graders. When she's not writing, she's crafting with her three children, sewing her own clothes, and snuggling with her cats. Sarah Marie lives in Belmont, Massachusetts. This is her first novel.